« *C A C T U S   T H O R N* »

Western Literature Series

Western Trails: A Collection of
Short Stories by Mary Austin
selected & edited by Melody Graulich

Cactus Thorn
by Mary Austin

A Novella by Mary Austin

CACTUS

with foreword & afterword by Melody Graulich

THORN

University of Nevada Press Reno & Las Vegas

Western Literature Series Editor:
John H. Irsfeld

Cactus Thorn *is reproduced by permission of*
The Huntington Library, San Marino, California.

The paper used in this book meets the requirements of American
National Standard for Information Sciences—Permanence of Paper
for Printed Library Materials, ANSI z39.48-1984. *Binding materials*
were chosen for strength and durability.

University of Nevada Press, Reno, Nevada 89557 USA
Copyright © University of Nevada Press 1988
Foreword and afterword copyright © Melody Graulich 1988
All rights reserved
Printed in the United States of America

Library of Congress Cataloging-in-Publication Data

Austin, Mary Hunter, *1868–1934.*
  Cactus thorn.

  (Western literature series)
  Bibliography: p.
  I. Title. II. Series.
PS3501.U8C3 1988   813'.52   88-10637
ISBN 0-87417-135-0 (alk. paper)

I N 1888 an ambitious but insecure young woman crossed the plains with her family and settled in the arid regions of southeastern California. There, in the "naked space," she cast off conventional ways of thinking, inadequate in a "country [that] failed to explain itself," a country that left her "spellbound" with "wanting to know." [1] And she learned to reject the capitulations of what she called "young ladihood." She made the "revolutionary discovery" that her life was her own, to live fully and freely. Her desert wanderings, and her encounters with the various "outliers" she met there, nourished her independence and rebelliousness: the desert gave her "the courage to sheer off what is not worth while" while "its treeless spaces," she discovered, "uncramp the soul." [2]

Austin spent fifteen years in what she called the "Country of the Lost Borders," seeking "a lurking, evasive Something, wistful, cruel, ardent; something that rustled and ran, that hung half-remotely, insistent on being noticed, fled from pursuit, and when you turned from it, leaped suddenly and fastened on your vitals" (*Earth Horizon*, 187). Although she would live, as a successful writer, in artist communities in Carmel, Greenwich Village, and London, the desert had become a part of her. She returned to the southwest for her final years, 1924–1934, borrowing an image from the Zia Indians to express the desert's lingering fascination: throughout her life, she said, she had sought the "Earth Horizon . . . the incalculable blue ring of sky meeting earth which is the source of experience" (*Earth Horizon*, 33). To Austin, as to Georgia O'Keeffe, the desert simultaneously revealed the mysterious and the "bare core of things" (*The Land of Little*

Rain, 8), "exciting in the heart that subtle sense of relationship to the earth horizon which is the nurture of the spiritual life" (*Earth Horizon*, 33).

In the desert Austin found not only personal liberation but also a voice and a subject matter. In many works she described how Native American women artists, desert storytellers, and landscape shaped her art. Beginning with *The Land of Little Rain* in 1903, she published a series of books which explored her most cherished theme, the influence of the desert landscape on human character, culture, and art: *The Basket Woman* (1904), *Lost Borders* (1909), *The American Rhythm* (1923), *The Land of Journey's Ending* (1924), *Starry Adventure* (1931), and *Earth Horizon* (1932), among others. When she wrote that the desert is "a land that once visited must be come back to inevitably," she was describing both literal and imaginative journeys (*The Land of Little Rain*, 5).

Cactus Thorn is another of Austin's imaginative journeys into the desert. A story about the relationship between a male politician with "new" ideas, the kind of man Austin encountered during her years in New York, and a self-sufficient woman wanderer, it has many autobiographical undertones, and it certainly reveals the point of view that made her one of the foremost feminists of her time. Although it has never been published before, it ranks with Austin's best writing and treats recurring themes which illuminate her career, as discussed in the Afterword.

Apparently written in 1927 and rejected by Houghton Mifflin, the novella remained in manuscript in The Huntington Library's Austin collection until this publication. The manuscript is unedited and includes typographical mistakes, misspellings, and inconsistent punctuation. Our intention was to limit editorial work to repairing these problems, but along the way we found a few sentences that required minor rewording to clarify meaning. Because we could not ask the author's approval for such changes, we modified the text only when absolutely necessary, making every attempt to preserve Austin's characteristic syntax.

We are grateful to The Huntington Library for permission to share this fine story with Austin's growing readership.

Notes

1. Mary Austin, *Earth Horizon* (New York: Literary Guild, 1932), pp. 194–95.
2. Mary Austin, *The Land of Little Rain* (Albuquerque: University of New Mexico Press, 1974), pp. 78, 91.

« *CACTUS THORN* »

GRANT Arliss had made two or three turns about the station platform before he saw her. So drugged was his gaze by the naked glare of a land whose very shadows looked rusted by the sun, he could scarcely take her in, lovely as she was, as a separate item of the landscape. She must have been sitting just there in the shelter of the alfalfa bales when the construction train had dropped him a quarter of an hour ago, taking him in with that same wide gaze, incurious as an animal's, which dropped without a spark as it crossed his own.

Arliss had been two days laying the raw silences of the desert to his soul. Not too long for him to be struck with the quality of her detachment, but long enough for him to put it to himself that the astonishing thing was, not that he had found a young and beautiful woman there, but that having found her, she did not disturb for him the somnolent desert charm. She was less of an item in it than the dwindling hoot of the train from whose caboose he had just descended, or the slinking rails over which, sometime that afternoon, the belated Flier would pick him up again.

He passed her the second time, to find that by some slight shift of her personality she had contrived, as some wild thing might, to remove herself even further from the scant field of his attention. But in the very moment of recognizing this removal he found himself yielding again to the pressure of vacuity which held him to the contemplation of the land's empty reach, its disordered horizons, its vast, sucking stillness.

It was to secure for himself just this long, uninterrupted wait at the ramshackle station, from whose high platform ores had once been shipped to forgotten smelters, that he had used his name, not unknown even so far from New York, to have himself dropped there to await the belated Flier from the East.

What he found in the untenanted valley, rising far on either side into nameless, broken ranges, was so exactly the reflection of his inward state that he was able, in his pacing rounds, to forget the presence of the girl until the high wheeling sun drove him automatically to shelter. The stir she made, making room for him in the only possible seat among the miscellaneous crates and bales, brought to him afresh not only the singularity of her being there, in a situation which could not be supposed to be improved by the presence of an unknown man, but the greater singularity of his failure to respond to any suggestion that might lie in her beauty and their aloneness, beauty of the same sleepy smoothness as the land itself, isolation subject only to the interruption of the Flier three or four hours hence.

And yet, for all effect she had upon him, she might, like the horned lizard starting from under his foot, have assembled herself from the tawny earth and the hot sand, or at a word resolve herself into the local element.

So absolute was this sense of her being a part of the place and the day that it was with the effect of going on with a suspended conversation that she presently addressed him.

"I wouldn't, if I were you," she suggested quietly, "not unless you are used to it." Forgetting why he had sat down, Arliss had made a restless movement to resume his pacing. To hide the start she gave him, he squinted upward toward the hot, shallow heaven.

"Isn't it safe?" he wished to know.

"Over in Pahwahnit," she said, with vague pointing movements of her throat and chin, "days like this, men drop dead with water in their canteens." Arliss remembered hearing of this.

"I didn't know Pahwahnit was so near." He looked with interest toward the low, mottled ranges which the girl had indicated.

"Oh, *near!*" she smiled. "It would be a good horse would take you to Pahwahnit in three days, from here. And your friends might be a month finding you."

"Ah," he became whimsical in turn, "that would suit me!" She gave him a moment of grave appreciation.

"It sure is a good country to lose yourself in."

Arliss reflected that this might well be a preliminary to finding yourself, which was what he had come West to do.

"The point being, of course," he said, "that there should be people interested in looking for you."

She considered this literally. "There's a ranch at Bennet Wells," she enumerated, "and two men doing assessment at the Bonnie Bell. Then there's always likely to be *vaqueros*. And the Indians. Only the Indians wouldn't know you were lost unless you told them. They would think you were simply taking a *paseo*."

"Ah, then," Arliss insisted, "there *are* people who manage to live here."

"Oh, live! If you can call it that!" she flashed at him. "People don't really live here: they just happen along and stay." She seemed to keep pace silently with his thought, which made a backward cast toward ancient uses of the desert. "Of course," she began again, "if you've got something to think out—" and then at his quick recognition of the personal touch, by the same subtle means which he had sensed earlier, she momentarily withdrew herself. Arliss felt himself remanded to the traveler's impersonal claim for information.

"I mean, would it be possible to get food and housing for a few months, while you *are* thinking it out?"

She nodded. "There's a sort of a town between those two ranges that look so close together; and ranches scattered about. It's a question really of water. When you have water you can have anything you want. *Any*thing!" She appeared to measure him a moment before selecting the confirming incident. "There was a man had an Italian villa here once: Over there, at Hawainda."

Arliss could just make it out, a scar on the furthest range where the crude reds and ochers of the plain altered subtly to pearl and amethyst, and the rusty shadows began to creep from under the heavy glare, and to fill the passes with blue drift.

"They say the very stones were brought from Italy, and marble seats and fountains for the terraced gardens, packed in by mule back—that was the story."

"There would be a story," Arliss agreed, "*and* a woman." It was the first note of sophistication he had ventured, and her low, amused laugh was the measure of her response.

"Three of them," she agreed. "His wife and two daughters. *They* had had about all they could stand of the desert when Beasley struck it rich; and he built the villa after they had been a year in Italy. He couldn't imagine what else it was they wanted. There's been no one there for years now, except Indians. They wouldn't live in the house, of course; they're superstitious. But they keep up the water pipes and the reservoir, I've heard, so they can play with the fountains."

"Oh, not really! Everybody *told* me I should find romance in the West, but I hadn't expected anything so good as this."

"Is that what you call romantic?" The girl frowned slightly to herself. "The Beasley women hated it, I've heard. They didn't lose any time getting out of it when the old man died. I suppose," she considered, "a thing can't seem romantic when it's the only thing that ever happened to you . . . there must be plenty of empty houses in New York that aren't in the least romantic."

"Ah," cried Arliss, caught, "how did you know I am from New York?" and immediately perceived that he had touched too nearly on that instinct by which, like some delicate insect, she took a sudden color of aloofness from the soil.

"There's a lot of Easterners out here every year," she let fall from behind the veil; "we get so we can pretty generally tell where they come from."

The check, if it amounted to that, was one that Arliss refused to admit, all the more because of the implied fatuousness of his momentary hope that she might have recognized him. It wasn't unlikely; he had many followers in the West and his picture was one of the stock cuts of contemporary news. But he was not so fatuous as not to feel, in the moment of perceiving himself still unknown, a measure of the freedom he had come so far to find. He returned, as far as possible, to the note of detachment in his next question. "And just where *have* we come? Where am I now, in respect to places one hears of—Los Angeles, for instance? And how would I go to that place—where the villa is?"

"Hah-wah-eenda," she pronounced with the soft southern roll. "It's an Indian word for 'Place of the Doves.' There was always water there, and they built their nests—You'd have to go by train from Los-Ahng-lace," again she gave him the soft, informing drawl, "to Barstow, I guess; and from there to Minnietta, it's two days by pack train, and then north across the long arm of Mesquite . . ." But already Arliss's interest had dropped. By the very vastness which her use of names and distances implied, he was beguiled again into that vacuity of mind which in his present situation of spiritual exhaustion appeared to him as the happiest state.

After a perfunctory question or two he found himself, this time unwarned, resuming his aimless round, and by a vague impulse of propriety, extending it down the track and around the point of an ancient lava flow, temporarily out of sight and sound of his fellow islander. Here, for an hour he so successfully maintained his wished-for detachment that until he came in sight of her again he was hardly aware that he had turned his steps back toward the station shed. She had risen and was moving about with a familiar definiteness which, by the aid of a white napkin spread upon a bale of hay, and the inward prompting which had turned him back upon his path, he recognized as meal getting.

Arliss had made no provision for himself during the long hours which must elapse before he could reach the dining car of the Flier, and the way in which she had taken this for granted in laying places for two at her improvised table struck him as one more item in the complete identification of the young woman with the place and the day. In a country in which the whole machinery of impulse and foresight is sucked out of a man, it is natural that food should simply appear.

She had produced, doubtless from some place where they were stored for just such emergencies, the simplest of equipments for making tea, and only waited for him to fetch water for it from the nearby tank, to include him in her arrangements.

"Your train may be late, you know," she had opposed to his conventional hesitancy over her proffered hospitality. It aroused him for the first time, by the implication of its not being her train also, to a question; since it was not to take the only possible train, what in the name of desolation was she there for? Not venturing to ask, he filled the extemporized kettle and placed it over the fire she had kindled amid the aimless wheel tracks at the back of the station.

It was a little past noon of the clock, that magical moment when the shadows begin to stir and crouch for their evening assault upon the plain, and the burnt reds and the thick yellows and pale ash of the desert clear and flash into translucent flame. In such moments one perceives the lure of the desert to be the secret lure of fire, to which in rare moments men have given themselves as to a goddess. While it lasted it seemed to Arliss that the whole land leaped alive from the kindling of their wayfaring hearth. It leaped subtly almost to the surfaces of this pale brown girl, as if she were, like the land, but the outward sheath of incredible hot forces that licked him with elusive tips before they dropped to the crackle of twigs under the kettle on the bare sand. Turning to gather a handful of fuel, he found the thin flame-colored film of a cactus flower almost under his fingers. Before the girl's sharp, deterring exclamation reached him, he drew back his inexperienced hand, wounded with the cactus thorn.

"There's only one way to admire a cactus," she commiserated, and while he fumbled for his handkerchief to swathe his pricked fingers, she held up the delicate blossom on the point of a dagger that she had produced unobtrusively from somewhere about her person.

"I didn't know that the thorns simply jumped at you like that," Arliss apologized, taking the proffered dagger, not so much to admire the sun-rayed flower as to wonder at the implement on which it was impaled. It was slender like a thorn and had a carved ivory handle which had been broken and mended deftly with bone. He wondered where she carried it and what provocation would have brought it leaping against himself.

"I suppose," he said gravely, handing it back to her, "that this is a typical desert experience; to admire and be stung."

The girl laughed, laying the flower back in the shade of its parent leaf and half consciously heaping a little sand over the severed end of the stem. "The desert's got a worse name than it deserves," she defended; "there's ways it has to be lived with—I suppose you'd be just as likely to be killed crossing Fifth Avenue if you didn't know the rules."

"Well," he admitted, "New York can sting you to death, too. But one reads—all sorts of things about how the desert lays hold on a man and never lets go."

"Oh, yes, it gets them. It seems to *want* people." She considered the wide, untenanted spaces, the rich promise of the soil. "It wants them too much," she concluded. "It is like a woman, you know—that has only one man or child: she loves it to death."

"That," said Arliss, "is positively the most alarming thing I have heard about it." She seriously agreed.

"There's accidents, of course, like missing the trail or getting out of water. But they are likely to happen to you anywhere. The desert sort of sucks you empty and throws you away. That is, unless you are willing to take what it gives you in place of what you had."

"Then it does give you something?"

"Everything!" she averred. "Only . . . you can't pick and choose." She turned back to an earlier phase of their conversation. "If you had come here to think something out, you know. Well, you won't."

"Won't think?"

"It will be done for you. Like a piece of knitting that you've got all wrong. It's taken out of your hands and unraveled; all you have to do is watch it being set right."

"Then I have come to exactly the right place!" He tried for the note of lightness to cover a certain dismay. For the one thing he knew he hadn't come for was to have things taken any more completely out of his hands. It was, he himself would have said, to get his thinking thoroughly in hand again, to restore his lost sense of ascendancy over a situation which, for the moment, impressed him as having points in common with the trackless land whose horizons were lost in illimitable disordered ranges.

He was sitting on the bare sand beside his companion who, for the purpose of tending their kettle, had dropped there with a lithe unconsciousness of habit. The homely occupation gave him a more direct sense of her personality than he had yet received. More a woman than a girl, he decided—twenty-three or -four, perhaps—but of her experience nothing could be judged. There was nothing Western about her as he had learned to recognize Westernness in current fiction. Her dress, the hat and the jacket of which she had laid aside, was such as the more competent of city stenographers might have worn.

But even while he speculated, she had turned from him in one of those lovely poses the secret of which was known only to the early Greeks, and poked at a greyish spot of earth with a stick. It looked a little firmer, perhaps, than the surrounding sand. Then to his amazement, the spot gathered itself together and scurried off toward the shelter of the cactus thorns. For a moment the spiked, squat head was held alert, the broad body pulsating with startled life, quieting slowly as the little creature dropped back upon its belly and, with a slight burrowing motion, became again a part of the sun and shade-mottled sand.

"I guess they have the right of it," the girl commented with one of those occasional odd lapses into colloquialism which Arliss had already speculated over. "They never start any knitting of their own. They take it all out in making themselves a part of the big pattern." She dropped the stick, and with a beautiful half turn toward the open country, took the measure of its vastness in her speech. "That's the best thing you get out of the desert. It teaches you never to make anything up. Like . . ." this time she searched the wide earth for comparison, "like marriage is with us."

This was the sort of thing that, said in the circle to which Arliss was accustomed, would have cleared instantly for the speaker an advanced position on the Freudian premise. It should have led, by way of "complexes" and a discussion of the Russian realists, to precisely the breath-shortening crisis from which it was supposed to tear the veil.

Said as a preliminary to the announcement that the kettle had boiled, it had the effect of one of those inadvertent gestures by which, in the middle of the game, the board is suddenly cleared. It left the other member of the engagement with hand extended and no piece to play.

Without waiting for an answer, apparently without expecting any, she took up the kettle and, leading the way back to their improvised table, gave herself to the administration of hospitality and the simple enjoyment of the meal. On her feet and moving she was even more beautiful than Arliss had at first conceded, and less provocative, an effect that was heightened by the girl's failure to make of the primitive ritual of fire and food, man and woman in the wilderness, the note of sex appeal. Evidently she found nothing in their situation to inhibit this casual introduction of a topic they were both young enough to approach with trepidation. He had to admit to himself, however, if any such trepidation existed on her part, it was admirably concealed. He found himself under the necessity of reviving the topic himself, if he was to discover what, if anything, she had meant by it.

"So you think," he suggested, "that marriage is made up."

"On one side or the other," she agreed. "I have seen the wild creatures mating, and I've never seen them unhappy in it. But I've seldom seen humans where one or both of them wasn't suffering, because they had already made up their minds beforehand that marriage ought to be something it hadn't turned out to be with them. That's what I mean about the effect that the desert has on men. If you come into it with your mind made up as to what you want to get from it, you may not get anything."

"But," Arliss expostulated, "when we go after anything we have to begin where we are."

"No," she shook her head thoughtfully. "You have to begin where *It* is. Like I said with marriage. You have to begin with what loving is, and cut your marriage accordingly. It's like a match and a piece of wood. After they come together you can't treat them any more as wood and match, but as fire, and deal with them according to the nature of fire."

"And if the fire goes out?" Arliss had that instinctive fear of the irrecoverable nature of marriage which manifests as a covert curiosity.

He was still far from admitting that his fear was the obverse side of an incapacity so far to make the wholehearted approach, but he had begun to wonder whether the mystery of his waning appetite for leadership, his reluctance to accept the opportunity held out to him, for fear his interest in its exercise might not hold out, were not of the same nature as the evanescent flame of passion. With that uncanny prescience for the trend of his secret thought which he had already noted in this singular young woman, his companion pointed her contempt with a glance at the burnt ends of sticks from which the flame of their own fire had already receded.

"There's ways of handling fire," she said. "You can spend all your time keeping it going, or you can build it up fresh when you need it from the coals. That's what I meant by being made up, when it ought to be something that exists that is there all the time, like a well, or," she reverted to the earlier figure, "like a fire in the depths of the earth, or fire in the sun. You oughtn't to have to keep poking at it to make it burn."

"Ah," he said, "I thought it was the business of women in particular to keep the fire burning . . . priestesses of the flame."

She took him in again with that incurious animal-like gaze. "You would," she said, with an impersonal finality that made Arliss aware that, thought he had never so stated it to himself, that was exactly what he had long wished to think. He knew that he had been thinking of marriage for himself as a possible way out of his present state of spiritual insufficiency. If only he could find a woman who could be counted on to kindle a flame and keep it going, he might, at that glow, warm the slowly chilling reaches of his intellect and his ambition. He had a momentary panic that this strange young woman, in placing him so accurately on one point, had also penetrated to the place of the chill and discovered what he had left New York to hide. Before he could, however, frame any sort of answer to this pointed judgment of himself, his companion had flicked the personal element from it with the shaking out of the crumbs of their meal, and was going on with her own thought. "I suppose," she half mused, "that's one of the ways in which women got sidetracked. They didn't *have* to keep making up the fire all the time, the way men do. They *lived* in the flame until men got to think of them as being makers of the flame. . . ." She dropped off with such complete disregard of her companion that for a moment he failed to follow her into simple comment on the country, the climate, the trails that went white and blind across the baked land.

Arliss was conscious of a vague irritation with this singular young person who "talked sex"—that was the way it was phrased in Arliss's own circle—and dropped it in that calm way just as the man was beginning to get interested. He would have liked to keep on with the subject, to point his protest against her reading of the function of woman as priestess of the flame, by his own need to feel the flame, any flame, for just the kindling touch which he was beginning to imagine she might have given, and so negligently refused. Here were all the materials of a fire—the romantic setting, the woman with her satisfying contours, the shadows of her hair like rusted gold, the fruity brownness of her skin. He had been astonished that she did not move him more at the beginning of their acquaintance and now he found himself vexed in the discovery that her mind was not even on the business of whether she moved him or not. His annoyance, however, was not deep enough to be proof against the simple charm of her talk, friendly and impersonal as a boy's, charged with all a boy's interest in and information about the region in which they found themselves marooned. Gradually his mind loosened its tension and ran out happily on the track which her talk provided.

At the end of an hour he was startled by the wild hooting of his approaching train in the narrow cañon to their right. The girl stood up, beginning to assemble her belongings with instinctive feminine movements of setting herself to rights. Arliss rose also, and for want of anything else to say, expressed the conventional hope that they were continuing their journey together.

"Oh, no!" she told him; she was expecting friends who would come for her—she threw a casual glance back toward the encircling hills and took the position of the sun—in another hour. And as she stood serene in her utter lack of any need of him, that happened which by every calculation of social incidence should have happened in the beginning. As at the striking of a match Arliss felt himself swept suddenly by the need of her, the need of a man for a woman, as natural as the need of water and as necessary as bread. She stood buttoning the ready-made jacket that fitted her lovely curves as it might have fitted the bronze Diana pointing her perpetual arrow within view of Arliss's New York office. Her brown eyes, pale brown like the shadows under the sage, smiled at him with the first glint of natural coquetry.

"I've been very happy to meet you, Mr. Arliss," she said.

"Ah," he cried, "I didn't tell you that!"

"Well, couldn't I just have seen your picture in the papers? It's there often enough."

There was so little to say to this that for the moment that was left to them amid the approaching thunder Arliss let his glance roam over her hungrily, until in passage it crossed her own for an instant in which she took the measure of his desire and disallowed it, as the cool surface of a statue might for a moment reflect, without being warmed by it, a passing torch. She clasped the hand which he formally held out to her, and shook it gravely. "Good-bye," she said, and again, "I'm very glad to have met you!"

« *T W O* »

CAUTION, and the average American idealism in which he had been brought up, had so far kept Arliss's adventures with women discreet and largely tentative. Years of European travel had freed his thinking of the limitations of his upbringing without involving him in the current European smudginess on the relations of the sexes. It had not, however, rid him of a disposition to think Americanly of all that passed under the head of "sex" as rather explicitly set apart from marriage—such a marriage as he had at the back of his general life purpose an intention to achieve. There had been no time, since his return from Europe, for him to bring that purpose to fruition in the career which his natural ability to speak persuasively, his easy knowledge of European conditions, and the contemporary stagnation of American politics had opened to him. And as he moved along the rising curve of that career, he had been increasingly sensible that his freedom from any disposition to make over the marital relations of society had been an important item of his success in suggesting that it could be made over politically. More and more he had found, in the general collapse of prewar radicalism, his unimpeachable private record ranking with his unencumbered private income as a political asset. It was only within the past year and a half that Arliss had begun to wonder if his moral impeccability was as much of an asset as it had formerly seemed.

In the interval of spiritual lethargy following the Peace Conference, Arliss's had been almost the only voice of hope and faith raised among that wasted generation who found their own hopes and faith deflated by the dust and ashes of participation in a war as unacceptable as it proved inconclusive. With a courage which bore no conscious relation to the stable quality of his income, Arliss had withstood both the fever of participation and the sloth of after-war relaxation. His views had been so right, with a kind of rightness appreciated by people who have no other guide than their own right feeling, that Arliss himself had never questioned the arrival of the inspiration for right doing, coincident with the opportunity. He had lent himself therefore, happily, to the pressure of his frankly uninspired following to the extent of being about to be pushed into a position in which the rule for right doing would be publicly required of him. And swiftly, with the opening of the door on what seemed to be the straight road to political leadership, Arliss discovered that the fire had gone out of him. It began to go with the necessity for repeating himself incessantly on the platform; it slipped from him like an expiring flame when in conference he struggled vainly to produce the programs of political action that were on every side demanded of him. He had no program. He could have managed without that. Political programs were, or should be, the spontaneous outcome of political interest in operation. The insuperable secret difficulty of Arliss's own soul was that he suffered a steady diminution of political interest.

It had been, in the beginning, much in Arliss's favor that he had never committed himself to any of the political and sociological superstitions that had been hung about the neck of that mythical angel of social redemption, the Social Revolution. He had been neither Anarchist, Communist, Socialist, Syndicalist, nor an adherent of any of the codified sociological solutions. And yet by the rumpus he had somehow managed to kick up about the existing political system in the United States, he found himself wholly committed to the necessity of defining, if not of initiating, a new system which should justify him in his original protest.

There had been nothing the matter with his original proposition that what America needed was pure politics based upon intelligent comprehension of her situation. There had, in fact, been too little the matter with it, too little to keep off the crowds of followers who appreciated such a proposition as an ideal, without having the least notion of how to constitute it as a practical reality. And after ten years of careful building up to the point at which political leadership lay within his grasp, Arliss made the disconcerting discovery that all he had so far done and said were based upon a state of mind, a state of feeling, which he found himself less and less able to maintain.

It was at this point, before he had admitted the difficulty even to himself, that Arliss began to wonder whether his own impeccability wasn't somehow the seat of his difficulty.

In the circle of immediate disciples, who had rather chosen themselves out of their own unorganized political anxiety than been chosen, "experience," by which was usually meant the sex adventure, was credited with the inestimable quality of nourishing the flame of life. Most of the men on whom Arliss depended for organized support entertained liberal views; the women—and his following was, if anything, larger and more enthusiastic among women than among men—not only had views, but were perfectly willing to let it be known that they had had "experience." Although there was nothing in Arliss's temperament to gild the irregular life for him, in his dryness he had begun to envy the experimental freedom of those members of what he had himself aptly termed the guerrilla warfare of social reform. If he had not sought release from his unfruitful state in such personal connections as were quite freely offered a man in his position, it was largely the fault of the women from whom such connections could discreetly be had. What Arliss wanted was to be filled again, to be warmed and quickened, to be raised to the level of personal competency from which he could again command his own career. And the difficulty with such women was that they wanted not to make Arliss competent to live his own life again, but to live that life with him and by means of him. They wanted to furnish ideas, organizing power, sensible aid; and all that Arliss wanted was that elusive quality of self-inflation called inspiration. This was the commodity which women had traditionally supplied; but all those women of Arliss's acquaintance from whom emanated the faint aroma of a possibility of supplying it, wanted something in exchange; they wanted marriage, or they wanted an opportunity to express themselves in life. From both of these contingencies as well as from the possibility of being found by his constituency as empty as he knew himself to be, Arliss had, on the plea of overwork, fled westward.

And the first point of attention in that flight had been a woman. She was a woman as strange, as arresting in her quality as the thin bright cactus flower. Almost as stinging as the cactus thorn. She had moved him without any motion toward either marriage or toward the use of her as the instrument of his own career. For the moment, in her nearness he had breathed again the sense of life as a large occasion to which he felt himself personally equal. And she had produced an effect upon him to which he had begun to suspect himself immune; she had done so without either offering or withholding. With every recalling of that moment, he felt a returning pulse of power which, though it left her inviolate, left him equally unrebuked. Perhaps with a longer time . . . , he had no expectation of ever seeing the girl again; but in his berth in the Flier he kept tasting the moment over and over, as an intimation of what the West might do to him.

Which made it all the more disappointing to find that Los Angeles, where he arrived the following evening, bored him inexpressibly. Arliss had named that city as the terminus of his flight for no reason except that it was the farthest from New York, and that his married sister, who lived there, had often written him

teams from there to Agua Hedionda, and from there you could get some of these old pocket hunters to carry you to Minnietta where the Indians—"

"Wait a minute," Arliss was taking out his notebook. "I want to write that down."

« T H R E E »

A WEEK later Arliss found himself in a buckboard, driven down the soundless, well-sunned middle of Mesquite Valley by a half-breed answering to the name of "Mojave." They were bound toward a campoodie of seminomadic Paiutes at the far end of Mesquite, where, so Fernald's friends had said when they furnished him with the buckboard and driver, he would find one Indian George, custodian of the old Beasley place at Hawainda.

All day, since a blue dawn widening to an unremitting glare, they had come with no sound between them but the occasional chirrup of the half-breed to his mules and the soft grind of the sand beneath the wheels. Coil by coil as the wheels turned, Arliss felt his past slip behind him.

Already he was hypnotized by the glare, by the monotony of endless elusive lines of dry landscape, beyond being teased by the fruitless efforts of his mind toward vistas that would not open and answers that were not to be found. Now and then, across the unrippled surface of his somnolent fatigue, there stole like a fresh wind a stir of the anticipation of relief; a wind that seemed to blow from that region in which a lovely, sleepy woman tended a little lipping flame. Now and then, when in place of this wind of refreshment blowing on sequestered corners of his soul he received a scorching blast from the shadeless sand, it seemed to him utterly logical that the landscape should suddenly blossom into that flame and that woman. Then he would shake himself into a half-intelligent wonder over the possibility of actually finding her there in the neighborhood to which he was bound. From this he would fall to a very luxury of weariness, and a deep word-less thankfulness that he need no longer prick himself to think.

About four in the afternoon, when the glare lay upon him at its most intolerable, a round green blob appeared in the distance against the prevailing black rock. Mojave waked himself and his mules long enough to head them in that direction and to remark, "Campoodie. Injun George," before falling again into the swoon of monotony in which, apparently, desert errands were accomplished. Half an hour later, what looked like brown wasps' nests in the shade of half a dozen cottonwood trees resolved into wattled huts clustered about a shallow spring.

The negotiations for the services of Indian George as guide to Beasley's were conducted by Mojave in a language of soft clicking and hissing speech, which, as the population of the tiny settlement collected around the point of interest, apparently had to be begun all over again with each new accession to the audience. Indian George, it appeared, had a great deal to say at great length on the state of the weather, the painted horizon, the fleckless sky, which for some reason he regarded as inauspicious.

"He say he no like," Mojave at last translated; "he say what for you want to camp at Beasley's. He say damn poor place. He say more better you camp at Lone Tree Spring."

"You say because I damn well don't want to." The white man accepted the measure of clipped speech. Whatever the interpreter made out of this was the occasion of a monologue on the part of a middle-aged woman of large girth, who, by the guilty embarrassment with which she was listened to by Indian George, could have been no other than his wife. Mojave finally collected the sense of the argument in a question.

"She say how you know about Beasley's?"

"You say, my friend tell me." Arliss, recalling what he had been told about Indian superstition, added largely, "White man no afraid," which statement caused Indian George's wife to clasp her hand over her mouth with what appeared to be amused amazement.

"He say you gonna meet your friend there?" the interpreter translated with a fine detachment, the effect of which was heightened by the subsequent discovery that his services had been wholly superfluous.

"Yes, yes," Arliss snatched at an acceptable excuse, "tell him I go there to meet my friend."

"All right," and surrendering himself to the situation, with an English better than Mojave's, Indian George climbed into the buckboard and directed the expedition.

From Cottonwood the road wound back to the open mesa, and about an hour later turned sharply to a *corral de tierra*, a circle of low, treeless hills, across which the villa gleamed white against the leopard-colored slope.

It was a very modern sort of villa, pretentious in its stucco decorations, with the remains of what had been a handsome pergola crossing the front and disappearing around one end. Below it the whole slope of the hill had been terraced and planted, set with wide stairs and stucco vases, all involved now in a clean, dry desolation.

The house had a waiting air, biding the desert's time. An ancient air adopted from the hills, as a good servant takes the note of a long-established dwelling. Here and there an orange tree or an oleander on the terrace survived meagerly, and a rose vine across the broken pergola waved a bright rag of bloom. Clean sand drifted against the terrace walls and overflowed the urns. Bunchgrass and cactus pried the stones apart.

The buckboard drove up from the front and deposited Arliss's baggage on the last terrace under the pergola. Green shutters guarded the windows and the door had been securely nailed across. Just outside the paved level of the upper terrace, some earlier camper had left the traces of a fire, to which it was evident the wooden supports of the pergola had contributed.

The bent but unrusted nose of a hydrant showed at the terrace edge. Mojave searched it out and turned the faucet easily. It ran a thread of water, cool and clear.

"Best water between here and Pahwahnit," he averred. "Some prospector he clean out reservoir some time maybe. Pretty good job." Arliss understood that this was an assurance that the water was safe and sweet, but for caution's sake he let the hydrant run while he laid out his belongings. He could hardly explain why he postponed any further exploration of the premises until he had seen the buckboard disappearing over the low barranca that fenced, without shutting in, the *corral de tierra*. The whole place carried, not only by association but by something in its clean detachment from himself and its easy acquiescence in the environment, a suggestion of the girl, a suggestion which he felt now he must guard as the only thing he was to have of her.

He told himself it was absurd that he should have allowed himself to imagine finding her here, and as the dust of Mojave's wheels died down and left the landscape empty, he told himself it was even more absurd that he should have come. He walked toward what had once been an orchard and noted that the house was so built as to form three sides of a court of which the fourth side was the smooth upslope of the hill. Within that court must be the fountain of which the girl had spoken, but he felt an odd reluctance to visit it. Presently, as the day began to drop, he heard the doves; the swift flirt of wings and the voices, round and tender as the light that filled the hollow of the *tierra*.

It occurred to Arliss that he had better have his supper before the dark fell, and it was then that he made a discovery. The trickle of water that ran from the open hydrant was finding its way along a well-defined channel to the roots of the rose. It had not yet reached the end of its channel, but the soil around the rose stem was dark with damp. It had every appearance of having been watered well and recently. This discovery gave another aspect to the shut dwelling, which already had begun to have for him that suggestion of the sinister which is so characteristic of abandoned houses, as though all that the inhabitants had been able to leave behind was the worst of themselves.

Postponing his meal, Arliss passed under the pergola, around the other side of the house, and through a wide passage into the court, along the upper end of which the pergola continued.

The first thing he saw there was, as he had expected, the ruined fountain, and beyond it, what might have been a garden merging at the far side into the hill. And immediately his attention was arrested by signs of recent occupancy. The back doors were shut and the curtains drawn at the windows, but two or three rococo and somewhat damaged pieces of furniture had been pulled together under the pergola, and on a table in a dish were half a dozen of the filmy flowers of the prickly pear. He recalled where he had first seen and admired them, and on a sudden impulse bent to examine the thick top of the disk which had been neatly sliced off with its flowering cluster. He looked for and found the mark of a small sharp implement on which they had been handled. And immediately the sudden leap of his fancy dropped cold. After all, he quoted to himself, "there's only one way to admire a cactus."

Plainly, however, the place was inhabited, and by some person or persons who had more right to it than he, since they went in and out and kept the key to the doors. He was inclined on the whole to be resentful at this intrusion, but felt better after he had cooked his supper over the blackened stones of the abandoned camp at the edge of the terrace. He had already gathered, from what he had heard, that the villa was a common watering place for all the region.

The sun had disappeared behind the ranges by the time he finished, and the day, as if it had but waited for that departure, dropped into a more leisurely pace. The *corral de tierra* and the long valley, which he could see beyond it, filled with lilac light that changed without lessening from moment to moment. The shadows between the hills lifted slowly and shook out their delicate veils.

Arliss found a path which led from the orchard into the one threading up from the back of the court, and followed it. Around him the whole earth swam in rose and violet; the trail was a thin ribbon of gold under his feet. And presently, as he knew now inevitably the whole place and hour existed to bring to pass, he saw her walking in it.

She came down from higher ranges, bareheaded, with a sheaf of crimson mallow in her arm, and an easy, homing stride. Arliss did not know at what moment she first spied him on the trail below her. He was anxious that she should see and recognize him before she came up with him, and with this in mind he walked out to the furthest edge of an intervening basalt outcrop, standing full against the light, and did not turn back into the trail until he heard the swish of her skirts against the sage. He did not know what to do then but to stand uncovered, offering himself to her decision.

"I saw you an hour ago, crossing the black rock," she said. "I thought it couldn't be anyone but you."

"But you can't suppose for a moment that I knew—that I came meaning to intrude," he stumbled into explanation. "I was so in need of some such place to—to think out something. And what you said about this villa appealed to me. I couldn't imagine you had selected it for yourself." He hoped she might not find that he protested too much. She considered the whole subject gravely before she said surprisingly:

"Do you want me to go away?"

"Dear lady! It is I who should talk of going. But you didn't give me the least idea that you were coming here."

"I hadn't the least idea myself," she said. "When you saw me at that station I was on my way to visit some friends that I hadn't seen for a long time. But friends change, or you change. The visit wasn't a success. And I'd been here before when I wanted—when I didn't know where else to go. Ah—look!"

By some magic of the afterglow, every hill turned translucent with secret fire mounting suddenly out of the earth's core. Overhead the heaven burned blue and the torch of a star flared white. The very air dartled and paled from flame to opal and took the stain of the colored earth like glass. The man and woman were caught up in it like souls translated.

"It is thinking of the time when it was all molten with the earth's fire," whispered the girl; "by and by it will begin to think of the time when it was blue with the sea from which it rose. Over there—" She pointed where the ancient shoreline showed white along the foot of the ranges. "They say the sea came in there not so very long ago. Times like this it comes back."

"I can see how it would come."

The wonder of it hushed their voices to a whisper. Silent, they watched the dream of fire die out of the mountains and the ghost of the ancient sea begin to steal in ethereal blueness along the bases of the hills.

The blue of the sky flowed, deepening, back into the middle arc, but above the mountains in a wide band it took on the silver pallor of a shell. Above it the thin, greenish rim of the new moon came out.

Arliss and the girl began to move along the trail which had widened sometime since to a wagon road.

"It goes up to the reservoir," she told him. "I've been up to see if there is anything I can do to start the fountain."

"You must know the place very well."

"Since I was a little girl My mother came sometimes to visit Mrs. Beasley. I was born and brought up, over beyond." She pointed in a direction opposite to the one from which Arliss had come. "They left the keys at our house and my father used to send their things as they wanted them. They were in such a hurry to get away they left the house pretty much as it was."

"I begin to see what an intruder I must seem."

"It's been years since they've even written," she assured him. "I doubt if anybody about here knows where they are. And the place is a common camping ground. The only thing you have to think about is whether my being here, as I am, makes it any the worse for you; gets in the way of your thinking, I mean."

"Dear lady," he began, not knowing what to say.

"It isn't," she added, "as if I didn't know how important what you think is to—to the rest of us."

"But," he protested, taking the whimsical turn in default of anything better, "I came here because I thought you promised that the thinking should be done for me. And seeing that I'm not even acquainted with the Powers who are so accommodating, I shall need you to introduce me to them, and," for he thought it high time he should have something to call her by, "to yourself also."

"Oh," she laughed an acknowledgment of his claim, and then oddly hesitated. "I go by my mother's name. Vallodón, Dulcie Adelaid Vallodón. Mother was Southern," she added, seeing him caught by its unexpectedness; "she thought a lot of names." Finally, after a pause, disposing of the whole matter of her identity, "My father's name was Kennedy." Presently, as they began to drop down into the dusk of the earth, while the tips of the ranges glowed still like molten glass, she began to inquire quite naturally of the incidents of his journey and arrival.

"I will have a room in the west wing cleared out for you tomorrow morning. My Indian woman comes every day about half past ten—" Arliss was reminded of something.

"Does she come from Cottonwood, and does she possess a husband who looks like Tutankhamen and answers to the name of George? Then unless you turn me out altogether, you will have to accept me on the footing of an old and valued friend." And he told her, making as light of it as possible, what had happened at the campoodie. He did not know in the least what ideas of propriety might attach, in exclusive Amerindian circles, to the meeting of a young and lovely woman and a solitary man, by appointment, a hundred miles from anywhere. He was so relieved to find that it evidently meant no occasion of embarrassment to the young woman.

"Indian George and Catameneda are among my oldest friends," she told him.

They found themselves compelled by the exigencies of the trail to walk in single file, and very little more passed between them except an occasional comment or precaution until they came up through the ruined garden past the fountain to the last terrace.

"Wait," she said, "I'll make a light."

He heard her fumbling along the wall while he stood still in the circle of his own dropping match, and presently she came back with a candle stuck on one of those oddly twisted bits of iron a miner uses to hang his candle to a rocky wall. By the pale flicker of the paraffin she seemed gravely to search his face. Between them and the table the flame-colored cactus flowers had delicately closed their rays. Arliss touched them gently, this time, mindful of the thorns.

"I hoped," he said with equal gravity, "when I saw those that I had found you again. I so greatly needed you."

"Yes," she said, and quietly as any hostess in a well-kept house she tendered him his candle. "I hope you will sleep well after your long ride, Mr. Arliss. Good night."

« *FOUR* »

URING the next week or ten days, Arliss was not without an occasional snigger from that little devil of sophistication which sits at the back of the male mind, interpreting women in terms of the lowest sort of use man has learned to make of woman. Here he was comfortably, if somewhat primitively, established in two rooms opening on the front terrace of the villa at Hawainda, and there was a handsome young woman, a girl in her early twenties, established domestically in two or three rooms at the back, with an unused but unlocked door and passageway between them, and no other person of their kind within two days' journey. He had a notion that the appearance of a new-built wickiup at the bottom of the orchard and the permanent establishment there of Indian George and Catameneda, his wife, might have been intended to constitute the local proprieties; and again it might have been only for the sake of what Arliss paid them to look after his rooms and meals. It was not until some-time afterward that he realized that the unobtrusive and competent way in which food and firewood and wild game simply appeared, his bed was made, and his belongings were always found ready to his hand, must have proceeded by the supervision of an orderly and foreseeing mind. The whole effect upon him was that he felt himself accepted by the land, free to absorb himself into its wide spaces and healing stillness. And except for the faint stir of conventional maleness in the mere fact of her being there, behind an unlocked door at the end of a passage, where occasionally he could hear her making a soft domestic stir early in the mornings or at night when she returned from *paseos* with the Indian women, he saw very little of Dulcie Adelaid.

He discovered that she was off with them occasionally for a day or two at a time, on errands she took no pains to explain; and on such occasions he discovered in himself an added sense of security and ease in the mere feminine flavor which the traces of her presence left in the patio and around the house. Rid of the vague disturbance of her unauthorized presence, he basked in the atmosphere of a simple domesticity created by the flutter of white curtains, the dish of flowers on the table under the vines, the occasional reminder of a hat or a shawl dropped upon a chair. On such occasions he would pace for hours up and down the terrace, or sit on the carved marble seat facing the ruined fountain, his pipe going out between his teeth and his mind happily caught away from immediate consciousness to the outer wheel of being.

By degrees he lengthened his walk around the *corral de tierra*, avoiding generally the path over the hill back of the house which was most used by Dulcie Adelaid, taking in the landscape as he walked, with the satisfied, undiscriminating gaze of a child, stretching down the long vistas glimpsed between the hills, or resting happily while watching, without conscious observation, a flower or a lizard basking in the sun.

On one of these occasions toward the end of his first week, he stumbled half consciously into a disused track leading out of the *tierra* and found himself at the end of an hour or two involved in a maze of round-backed hills, endowed with mysterious propensities for closing in behind and opening with false suggestions of familiarity before him. He walked on for a quarter of an hour before realizing that he was no longer able to decide whether he had or had not taken that particular turn, and then in an instant the terror of waste places was upon him. Mockery distorted the outlines of the hills; they bared their teeth. He ran, he tried to believe afterward that he had not shouted, at least not in utter fright. He was suddenly thirsty and immeasurably impotent and alone. And then, in the most natural way in the world, Indian

George appeared over the rim of a hill, rifle on arm and a pair of dead rabbits dangling from his hand.

Arliss was making an amusing tale of it that evening to Dulcie Adelaid, when at some delicate flicker of her glance it suddenly occurred to him that was precisely what George had been paid to do. His excursion and his fright alike were expected and prepared-for items of his desert experience. He was both touched and mortified by the discovery, and delivered unconditionally to her hand.

It was the very next afternoon that she asked him, for the first time, to walk with her to the reservoir, to discover if its condition would justify an attempt to rehabilitate the disused fountain.

The original Hawainda spring opened from a side hill above what had once been the orchard, and still in season ran a considerable rill of water, but the house had been supplied from a tunnel driven deep into the country rock, an hour's walk up the ravine from the garden. Fine white trails rayed out from it to all quarters of the hills, by which the small wild denizens came to drink. From the mouth of the tunnel they could see far up the range, between the reddish flanks of the cañon, the ruined scar of the mine.

"There's good ore there yet if it was mined right," the girl told him. "Beasley was really only a pocket hunter; he just about tore the insides out of the hill, getting at the rich streaks." Arliss found in her description his favorite indignation. That, he protested, was how men went about the earth, snatching and rending, and even as they tore at the hills for a handful of gain, they despoiled and exploited one another. Once he was launched on the social protest he slipped easily into the born politician's facility of denunciation, and quoted freely from himself. From the rim of the shadowed pool, the girl lifted her face to him in bright agreement.

"That's the first thing of yours I remember noticing," she said.

"When you said about the Child Labor bill that the freshness and beauty of youth was an asset to be cooperated with, and not to be exploited. It was in all the papers. A girl I roomed with in Los Angeles cut it out and stuck it in the looking glass. She'd been exploited herself since she was fourteen."

"Yes," Arliss agreed, "I could say that about child labor and get by with it. If I'd said it about mines and machinery they'd have called me a Socialist."

"You could say it about children," she insisted, "because women were listening to you. It's something women have been waiting for somebody to say. It's something they've always wanted known. About personal quality being an asset, I mean. That's what makes them suffer so when men mistreat them. It is because the thing in them that is injured is all they have to give. It—it lets them out of the game somehow to be—ruined." She hesitated naively over the old-fashioned words. Arliss frowned. He had been thinking of industrial despoiliation; he hadn't, any more than most men, comprehended that unification of woman's nature that leads her to see in every infringement an assault upon her femininity. He found it disappointing that this girl of the wilderness should exhibit the tendency that annoyed him so much in more sophisticated women, to "lead the subject back to sex," when it so clearly had to do only with economics.

"It's all nonsense," he declared, committing himself recklessly to issues he had hitherto been cautious to avoid, "for women to think of themselves as 'ruined' by a single experience. It's not a thing that establishes the criterion of conduct, it's the trend of behavior, whether it throws the individual up or down in the scale of social utility."

"Ah," she took him up brightly, breathlessly, "you said that about the Mexican Revolution, 'not that a bloody and violent revolution has occurred, but that the political energy of a people has been set free for constructive activity.'"

"Why, see here," Arliss was half flattered, half vexed, "we are going to run out of conversation if you know me by heart like that."

"Well, and if I didn't feel that I know you," she was gravely simple, "we wouldn't be having conversations like that, would we?" Was there, perhaps, a trace of anxiety in the voice, an effort to reestablish between them, on the ground of his public probity, the conventional exception from conventionality that women with whom he worked politically resorted to so annoyingly—the assumption that between a particular man and a woman a relationship could exist, a line of behavior initiated which was otherwise impossible, but between *them*, absolutely all right? Confound women! Why had they always to be so personal, "always bringing the subject back to sex." And immediately, as though she did not know the subject to have strayed, Dulcie unconsciously shifted the whole mechanism of his thinking.

"When I'm out with the Indian women," she said, "gathering roots and materials for basket making, it's not that I expect to make baskets or drink their medicine, it's the things you sort of soak up from the earth while you're with them, the things that make women wise. I don't know if I can explain—it's not as if they learned about willows and grasses in order to make baskets, but as if they learned to make baskets by knowing willows. I guess men used to learn that way once—learned to make bows by knowing junipers, the way their branches bend and spring back. But now they try to do all their learning in their heads." Again, as on that day of the shared fire and food she had the effect of rending, as by a lightning flash, the obscure cloud that rested on Arliss's mind. So that was what she was about on those inexplicable errands which took her out of his reach for days at a time—resorting to a primitiveness that was not the fierce, food-snatching struggle of the cave men of fiction, but a surrender to informing and creative intimacies with earth and fire and root and stone. And instantly with this lightning flash which she threw across the nature of women, as closer always to the moulding realities of earth, Arliss himself was taken with the intolerable homesickness of man for woman; to impenetrate, to be reabsorbed and wholly lost from himself in her. He did not know what he said, whether he said anything at all, but at her motion to rise he rose, holding out his hand to her, and was aware that he trembled.

It was after that that he found himself resenting her day-long absences, not so much because he objected to being left alone, as because she came back to him reinforced with strange powers she did not take the trouble to make him understand. He had a touch of that fear of the unknowable in her which is the root of sex antagonism.

At the hour when in the nature of things he could have expected her back, he found himself growing restless, walking the hills behind the house and concealing his desire for her company under a pretense of anxiety. On one of these occasions, when he had been about a fortnight at Hawainda, he had walked himself into that state which often overtakes men in an unoccupied land, his conscious mind traveling so far from his feet that his feet carried him inevitably as they had done the very first time of his walking there, by the force of his unconscious desire, into her homing trail.

It was well on into the long twilight when he caught sight of her, one of those hours that come only at the end of spring, when the sunlight, caught in an invisible web of atmosphere, makes itself molten, and spreads itself along the ground like gold. Overhead, the earth's penumbra was filled with pellucid dusk, shattered from point to point by the shrill cry of the nightjar. The girl came over the hill, free striding and empty handed, but not alone. Close at her heels trotted two of the little desert wolves, smut-nosed and pointy-eared. Scouting to one side but never forging ahead or falling completely behind, a full-grown female maintained a cautious distance. It was the half halt and lifted paw of this doubtful member that called the girl's attention to Arliss's presence in the trail ahead. At her gesture he stood still, scarcely breathing, until with steady approach she managed to bring two of her shy companions to his side. They moved altogether in the trail for an interval, but low as Arliss spoke, at the first whisper of a strange voice the little beasts trotted shyly out of reach.

"They can't be sure of you," she apologized. "Creatures that do not wear skirts are so likely to carry guns."

"Ah," the man protested. "You can't make me believe so easily that you do not carry a secret charm. They'd never follow me in a thousand years."

"They must have followed men once, or they wouldn't have become dogs. They are friendly little beasts really. Sometimes I think they are lonely for the old, kind time. It's in their voices."

Somewhere behind the hills there came a long, throaty whine, and then, further off, short yipping barks, held under the breath for caution. "There!" she half laughed, and then, at some nuance indistinguishable to the man's unpracticed ear, she pricked to attention. Signaling for silence she moved forward in the trail, and following her gesture without a word, Arliss found himself slumping quietly to the brown basalt that cropped out below them on the hill. He tried as much as possible to imitate the movements by which the girl adjusted herself to the blunt outlines of the rocks, leaning her head upon her arms to shadow the whiteness of her face and hands, glowing with an intensified pallor in the eerie light.

"Over the brow of the hill, there to the right," she breathed. Sharp against the skyline, but motionless, as if carved of stone, he saw the heavy-headed leader of the flock, straining to catch the tainted wind. From under the huge, recurved horns, the eyeballs, moving and alert, flickered over the crouching pair and swept the empty slope. Once, twice, the leader stamped his delicate hooves, and immediately the whole herd trotted up behind him, fell into line, and began to move steadily uphill. There were about a score of them, young rams and ewes with their lambs of the year before, almost indistinguishable against the twilit hill, except for the whitish undersides that flashed across the trail not a stone's throw from where Arliss and the girl lay.

"Mountain sheep," she said, when they had watched the lovely creatures out of sight, skimming like flying birds between the soft darkness of the earth and the pellucid darkness of the sky. "It's a sign the spring is over and the summer at hand, when they go to the high places."

"Are they always so unafraid?" Arliss spoke, whispering still, for the spell of the wild was on him.

"It's against the law to kill them. If I'd been alone I could probably have gone quite close to them. And if I hadn't been sure you had no gun, I'd have shouted to scare them. I was with a man once—he pretended he didn't believe I could take him close to them—and all the time he had a pistol hidden in his clothes!" She moved again into the trail, and with anger-quickened step. Arliss wondered what she might have done to that man, but forbore to ask. He recalled how at their first meeting she had drawn the sand over the severed cactus stem, and was moved with tenderness toward her as toward a child.

Evidently her day had tried her, for she was more than ordinarily silent at their evening meal, for by way of long walks and late returning they had fallen into a natural community of food; she came and sat beside him after it, on the marble seat among the artichokes, while Arliss smoked and the fountain's soft, incessant rain supplied the need of words. Finally the moon came walking on the hills and flooded the hollow of the patio with light.

"It will be at the full in a day or two," she said. "I must take you up on Ubehebe some night to see the moon mirage; it is often quite wonderful from there. We could take our blankets and what food we would need on George's pony."

"I should like that very much," he said, without once wondering what his circle would have said to this extraordinary proposal. The breath of her gentle wildness had blown out of him the last touch of that caddishness with which men habitually meet the unusual in women's behavior.

She did not, however, speak of it again. Whether because she had forgotten or because that mysterious prescience of hers for what was going on at any moment in any far corner of the hills had advised her that the hour was not right, Arliss did not ask. He accepted without question a later suggestion of an all-day ride to the ridge that cut the sky above the rift of the mine. From here they looked west across a knife-cut valley, and beyond a lower range that dropped by broken terraces to an alkali-whitened plain. Far at the end, under the heat haze, he could make out an oasis of citron green, deepening to what looked like a small plantation of alfalfa and orchard trees. A cattle ranch she told him, fairly good range and a great spring coming up in the midst of it like an artesian well.

"*Agua Dulce*, 'Sweetwater Ranch,' they call it"; and after a pause she added simply, "I was born there." It looked far and mysterious, like the sort of place from which she could have sprung. Sweetwater, the spirit of a wayfaring well.

"Dulcie—Agua Dulce—Dulcie Adelaid." She laughed as he tried out the aptness of her name.

"That was always the way my father would have it," she said, "but it was my mother's name really. My mother was—different. I think she ran away with my father from some better sort of life. Softer, I mean, more friendly."

Arliss brought the gift of sympathetic silence, which had made him notable, to bear on the hesitancy she seemed always to have in speaking of herself. "She died when I was fourteen, and I was sent away to school," she said. "It was then I began to call myself by her name. It was all I seemed to have of her. My father didn't mind." She seemed anxious on the point of his understanding that.

"It was a beautiful way of remembering," Arliss assured her. "It must have been lonely for you."

"Lonely! O—oh!" She gave a short, wounded, animal cry, the first flash of that fire which, from the day he had met her, he surmised behind her smooth surface. But before he could meet it with any answering warmth of his own, it had dropped like a half-drawn sword.

"I didn't live there after my father died," she said, with a note of finality which Arliss had no wish to protest.

Soft veils of heat began to draw between them and the oasis of Sweetwater. A wind from the top of the world played across the bunchgrass, the bridles of the cropping horses clinked softly behind them in the shade of the fox-tail pines.

"You know, the thing that bothered me most when I began to go about the towns, was finding out why they did things—all sorts of things. They seemed to me so—so made up."

"I remember you said that about marriage. That day at the station."

"I must have been thinking of my friend, the one I was going to visit. She wasn't very happy. Not because there was anything wrong, but because they both of them had made-up ideas that a husband ought to be this and a wife ought to be that. Well, it was *all* like that to me; society and religion and politics. They seemed to be trying to do it all themselves."

"But isn't that just the trouble?" Arliss wished to know. "They haven't done things themselves. They've taken other people's word for things; the church, the state, the party? Isn't that what we are trying to do for them, to teach them to think things out for themselves?" She shook her head slowly with a lip pinched thoughtfully between thumb and finger.

"The way you mean, perhaps. But not the way I mean. It is something you learn in a place like this. There is something here." She waved her arm over the wild disorder of the ranges. "It goes on by itself, doing things that you don't see either the beginning of, or the end, except that It has very little to do with men. It can use men, It *will* use them, but It can get on without them. They have to make themselves worth using.

"You remember what happened when you went walking by yourself? You were just thinking and thinking, weren't you? And suddenly you were lost. That was because you got away from— It. And then you were scared. But if you had waited, just held still and waited, It would have come back. You would have found yourself.

"There were things like that in the city to me. The people had gone off by themselves, and they were beginning to run around and shout to one another that this was the way, and this. But if they would keep still, the way would have come forth like a wild thing and shown itself."

"A month ago," said Arliss, "I wouldn't have known what you meant."

"It is because you were the only one who never seemed to say, 'This is the way,' that I believed you from the first," said Dulcie Adelaid. "My friend, the girl I told you about, was a Socialist. She said you'd have to come to it. But I knew better."

"You're right about that," Arliss agreed.

"I could tell," she triumphed, "by the way you kept off from all those things, that you *felt* there was Something, whether you knew what it was or not. I knew the minute I saw you get off that train that I was right, that I wouldn't need to make up anything with you."

It was very still where they stood on the very crest of the range; even the the wind had ceased to stir. Sweetwater lay hidden under a lilac haze, and over the vast assemblage of ranges rose far to the west a single snowy crest that seemed to float on the opalescent air. Save for their horses cropping in the bunch-grass, they might have been the only creatures in the world.

Touched, as any man might be, at seeing what he had secretly regarded as his worst weakness put in the light of a superior quality, Arliss was still a man of genuine kindliness. He distinctly meant not to do the girl a harm. He put out his hand over the firm, shapely fingers, "Dulcie Adelaid," he had not called her by her name before, "you mustn't make too much of me and what I stand for," he cautioned.

He found her more charming than he had ever known her, and for days after, their intercourse was marked by an increase of human ease and warmth. He thought now that he had her story, that he understood her, quite. He even had the grace to be ashamed of the suspicion which earlier he had entertained of her. If she talked to him as beautiful young women do not often talk to strange men, it was because after all he was known and identified as a man before whom nothing need be made up.

ABOUT a week after they had seen the wild sheep go over the top of the range toward the high pastures, when there had already come that change in the atmosphere that marked the final passage of the spring, they set out to walk to the mouth of Beasley's abandoned mine. It was a long, hot climb, for there was little air in the cañon, and the foot trail zigzagged brokenly up its chimney-like rift. The ruined tunnel, festooned with bats and adrip with mineral-stained waters, together with the general air of wreck and wastage, drove them by preference to seek the warm shadows of the *arrastra*, and after they had eaten their frugal lunch, to separate for the customary midday siesta.

How long he lay stretched on the steep slope with his hat over his eyes, Arliss did not know. The noon hush was still in the air and the rift was filling slowly with airy, afternoon shadow. Full of the languor of content, he lay still and began to call for his companion in his mind. With the friendly sense of proprietorship which his knowledge of her story—as he supposed—gave him, he had begun to play with her fine susceptibilities. He knew that if she was not too preoccupied, if he kept still, as he was doing now, and fixed his mind upon her, she would presently appear in his neighborhood. So, without turning, he lay and called wordlessly, "Dulcie, Dulcie Adelaid!"

Presently he heard further up the soft "Coo-ee" by which she notified him of her nearness, given tentatively, not to disturb his possible slumbers. Answering in the same key, he heard, a moment later, her light step. She was almost on him when he caught the arrested swish of her skirts, and then her voice, tense and compelling, "*Don't move!*"

"Don't move!" she said again, this time with a touch of wildness. Immediately the warning word was followed on his right by a warning rattle. Arliss felt himself grow pallid as he concentrated all his forces on keeping back the start of his muscles. He hoped to God he would be able to refrain from making a fool of himself.

"Be ready when I say 'jump,'" she whispered, and instantly there was a flash and a shadow across his face, and her voice crying, "This way! Jump!"

He was on his feet in time to see the rattler, pinned to earth by a small dagger like a thorn, twisting and thrashing.

They behaved very creditably while Arliss brought a stick and dispatched the snake and with the dagger detached the rattles for a trophy. They said it was careless of them both not to know that Arliss should not have lain down in the sun, now that summer was well on its way toward them. She explained how it was that snakes were so much more likely to be found in the neighborhood of water holes, and specially about old buildings where mice abound. Neither of them referred to what might have happened had Dulcie Adelaid been less cool and sure of aim. Arliss examined the dagger with care and thought it might originally have been of very ancient Spanish workmanship, as was shown by the handle, which had been mended several times.

Dulcie told him the story of how it had been given to her mother by a Mexican who had fallen in love with her, who taught her to use it as a protection, possibly against himself— "For who knows at what moment I may be unable to restrain myself, *señora mia*"—and later he had taught Dulcie, for the two women had both hated firearms.

"My mother made me promise never to be without it," the girl finished, "but this is the first time I have had to use it."

"I can understand that you would not." Arliss cleaned the dagger carefully on the sand and gave it back to her; it did not occur to either of them to turn away as she restored it to its sheath in her garter.

They were very silent going down and found themselves starting at unexpected sounds. They went back by way of the reservoir, to give variety to their excursion, and as they dropped into the last lap of the trail above the garden, the alpen glow had burned down to its lowest, insistent note of dusky red. There was a sharp break-off in the trail where it ended at the patio, and as Arliss turned back to offer his hand, it seemed to him as though her whole body had become a vessel of light. As he helped her down, she rested her hands upon his shoulders. "It might have struck you," she said, "it might—up there so far from help—it might have struck you before I could get to you." He held her till a gust of trembling passed. But he knew, when at her slightest motion to disengage herself he released her, that that thing had happened which he had supposed from the first must happen. Mysterious as she still was, lovely as from the first he had known her, she had become the woman of his desire.

They were very quiet at the evening meal that Catameneda had prepared for them. The candlelight flickered between them on Dulcie's pure contours and the white folds of her dress, for it was often her habit to change at evening from the neutral-colored garments of the day. Talk sprang up and died between them like the tiny puffs of air in the hollow of the patio. The moon came up and put the candle out. Arliss pushed back his chair at last and moved around the table to her. She gave him her hand, without rising, and he pressed it not knowing what to say, nor feeling the need of any words. Gently, at last, she withdrew her hand and Arliss went quietly out.

He said to himself that he must think, that he must come to some conclusion. A step one way or the other and this thing might become serious. But after a considerable lapse of time, he realized that he had not thought at all. He began to walk up and down under the long pergola, but thoughts did not come any more readily for that. He must have been an hour at least at that business, for he observed the heavens slowly filling with glory from the risen moon. Somewhere beyond the *corral de tierra* he heard a coyote call, as Dulcie had taught him to recognize, to its mate. He turned sharply and passed around the house into the garden. Against the marble of the fountain he could make out the gleam of her white dress. She put out her hand, half in defense, it seemed, as he came, and seizing it, he drew her slowly to him. All at once she surrendered, clinging to him and panting.

"Oh, my dear," she said, "I thought you would never come!"

IT was not very long after this that Arliss discovered that the fountains of his mind were broken up. Dulcie cleared him an upper room in the villa overlooking the *corral de tierra* and he began to devote a part of his days to the elucidation of ideas. It was no part of Arliss's method to give literary form to his point of view. He could write of explicit things he had done in a manner that detracted nothing from the achievement. For the "message" of social regeneration, which he was expected by his followers to deliver, he depended on the lecture platform. But before he could give it the final embodiment of voice and manner, it was his habit to hammer his thought out on paper, in structural continuity of terse, skeletal sentences.

For this purpose, he would sit long uninterrupted mornings, his gaze roving down the fawn- and lilac-colored vista of the *corral de tierra*, whose silence seemed to surround him like a flood, on the surface of which streamed toward him surprising intimations. Forgotten facts came drifting back from student sources, social incidents observed, but as yet unnoted, the flotsam of submerged experience. They bobbed and drifted on the current of his thought and betrayed an unexpected trend.

He found himself enormously interested in the process going on in himself. Sometimes whole mornings would pass with the white sheet before him still unlined, but without his experiencing any sense of wasted time. Other days the fires lighted by the friction of one dry uncertainty upon another would send him pacing in the hills until physical weariness drove him back to Dulcie and the relief of the long, half social, quizzing talks.

The girl listened inspiringly. Her reading had been unregulated but wide. Wherever it failed to bridge the gaps in his progressions, she had a way of dipping down into that mysterious wisdom which she shared with the Indian women, coming up with him triumphantly from point to point. He told her once that she used life like an encyclopedia, and immediately wrote down the phrase as one too good to lose, expanding it into a brief on the value of the common experience as social corrective.

"You *do* see through things," Dulcie had said to him when he read it to her, sitting under the rehabilitated pergola just before the noon siesta. And he had answered with something appropriate to the measure of illumination he had found in his relation to her. So it was that in their talk—a flare struck by the nature of their contact, lighting with many-colored jewel flashes the unsounded deeps of experience—they accepted the situation.

That he thought of it as something he had a claim upon, rather than as establishing a claim upon himself, was perhaps due to the girl's instinctive delicacy. There had been, even from the beginning, no bridal airs, no proprietary provocation. She never cheapened the flame-like quality of her surrender by lighting the kitchen fire with it.

Hitherto, Arliss's limited experience with women had been colored by the youthful atmosphere of escapade—and the more sophisticated precaution against the misadventure of being "caught." In the current phraseology of the circle in which he had been brought up, the whole business of women was to "catch" men and bind them to the uses of the family. He had been taught, expected naturally to have a wife and family of his own, securely established in all the social formalities, a fenced and valued possession. But he had always thought of this as something in a manner extraneous to his work, something to be added to it at the appropriate, enhancing moment. Among the women who in his public life had come closest to him, the object of catching a man was to use him as an instrument of personal expression. Nowhere had he learned of relationships with women which should enter into his life like bread and wine, the sustenance of being.

As the summer increased he and Dulcie walked abroad less, especially in the daytime, but nights often found them far from home, walking till they were weary and lying down until moon-rise on the warm sands. Sometimes they fell asleep there, waking to find the blue of the sky drawn into the vault beyond the earth's shadow, the planets swinging like lamps in their courses. Oftener they sat by the fountain, and while Arliss smoked, Dulcie would bring forth a guitar which she played not well, but pleasingly. Sometimes she would sing sentimental ballads that must have been part of her mother's repertory, or soft strumming Spanish melodies. Invariably, the sound of the guitar would bring the Indians up from their wickiups in the orchard, and they would sing altogether. Dulcie would strike a chord on her guitar and then would begin a long, swaying murmur, first one by itself and then another, with odd little discrepancies of time which over-took and caught one another up at intervals. Suddenly out of the dark there would rise the sharp yelping note of a sensibility tug-ging at its leash, and an answering rise in the whole throaty pack. Presently the music disengaged itself in figures of two or three notes, chasing their own tails in play until one of them dashed off in pursuit of some elusive melody which died finally amid the distant yelping of the pack. Then Dulcie would touch the guitar again, and from some happy hunting ground of the spirit the little tune would come back as a ghost and sing itself softly out to a humming accompaniment.

Once in a fortnight Indian George would disappear down Mesquite Valley with his rackety team, returning in three or four days with such supplies as were required.

Once a solitary prospector filled his canteen at the terrace hydrant and drifted off toward Ubehebe. A pocket hunter, with

two burros and a dry washing outfit, spent the night on the terrace. Dulcie was away at the time and Arliss, diverted as he was
by the man's oddities, was disturbed by his obvious curiosity over
Arliss's own situation, the more so as he detected in Catameneda's
maneuvers, as she brought him his supper, a determination to
present him to the stranger's eye as a solitary bachelor. Late, late
Arliss lay awake under the pergola with the stranger snoring below him on the terrace, straining his ears for a hint of the girl's
return. Fortunately the pocket hunter pulled out at daybreak.

Arliss undertook, in mentioning the pocket hunter's visit, to
convey delicately to Dulcie that he was very much in her hands
when it came to presenting their relation to outsiders, but in the
end he remained a stranger to her intention.

In August they took camp and established themselves on
Ubehebe, between the twin roundness of the mountain that is
called Maiden's Breast. Here a spring came out from under huge
stones in a flowery meadow. Sparse-limbed pines stood up, with
oaks, and here and there dark, browsing junipers. More than
once the mountain sheep fed in their meadow, and a puma came
at twilight to play with her yellow kittens around the spring.

Indian George, who had packed their goods in on his ponies,
was of the opinion that if they looked for them about the mountain's left breast, they might find deer. Dulcie proposed that the
Indian take Arliss for two or three day's shooting, but she could
not be persuaded to accompany him herself. "It would be wrong
for me," she insisted.

"Can it be," Arliss teased her, "that you are abandoning me to
evil practices?"

"Oh, you aren't a member of the desert tribe," she seriously
told him. She turned on him squarely in some surprise. "Haven't
you ever seen anything that made you think that there is a different kind of rightness for different kinds of people? If I were to go
against the wild things, something would happen to me."

"I've seen people do things that couldn't possibly be defended as right, and still not suffer for it," agreed Arliss. "That was what used to floor me so when I was young and believed in natural justice. Men could be the very fountainhead of economic corruption and yet die happy in their beds, their wives would be faithful to them and their children do them credit."

Dulcie turned this over thoughtfully. "It was because they didn't go against their Medicine, as the Indians say. It all goes with what I said before about being used. So long as we don't do anything to interfere with what is using us, anything to make ourselves unusable, I think It doesn't pay very much attention to us!"

"So you think I could kill a deer without calling down punishment, but there *might* be things I couldn't do?"

"Many things." It amused him to see that she was utterly serious. "It is your Medicine to spread justice and honesty into business and trade and society. If you went against that, if you—grafted, in anything, yourself, I guess you'd be punished for it."

Arliss turned lazily on the litter of pine needles where he lay and drew her soft palm across his eyes to keep out the sun. "You are a pagan, Dulcie," he declared, "rank pagan, and your gods are highly utilitarian."

"They've got to be, with the earth and all the worlds to attend to! Why should they bother about the little things we do for ourselves and each other so long as we don't get in their way?"

"Is that why—?" The question started out of Arliss almost unawares. He hoped he had stopped himself in time, but Dulcie was too quick for him.

"That's why," she affirmed, "I should be afraid to tell a lie or to kill a deer, but I am not afraid about us. What we are doing doesn't make us—nor anybody—unfit. Don't you *feel* I'm right?"

Curiously, that was the way he felt. He had had a good many revelations in the past three months, but the most astonishing was the way he felt about Dulcie Adelaid, the extraordinary kind of rightness the relation seemed to have established for itself. He began to understand why men as a group had resisted the absolute classification of their relationships into moral and immoral. Here was a thing which transcended definition and wove itself into the very texture of life. He did not even question the validity of his affair so far as to frame excuses for it. He had come home to the woman, after his excursions into sophisticated living, as he came back to the fire between two stones, the bed on the ground. And at the same time that the man in him was touched by the simplicity of her faith, the public character sensed the value of her quaint philosophy as a feint in that intricate swordplay of moral prejudices to which his platform life committed him.

Without actually accepting it for himself, he was struck with the use he could make of a concept of morality based on its suitability to the uses of the Powers. He came back to the subject from another angle.

"You think your gods wouldn't mind if I killed a deer; what would they do if I killed a man?"

"It would depend, I suppose, on how badly the man needed killing. Wasn't that your argument for the cotton strikers; that it was a matter of life and death with them?"

"It was war, and my point was that killing has always been justified in war, and by the very people who condemned the strikers."

"Well, I suppose there are private wars that are as excusable as wars about politics or money. Everybody has a right to a chance at life, and if anybody was spoiling my chance—making it so miserable I couldn't endure it—and there wasn't any other way of dealing with him—if it was something the law hadn't provided for, I mean—well, I wouldn't *let* him spoil it."

"Oh, Dulcie Adelaid," Arliss laughed, "how the Radicals would love you!"

"Will they?" she speculated hopefully, "I shall want your friends to like me."

The "will" and "shall" pricked warningly at his attention. It was not the first time Arliss had been struck by the necessity of considering what was to be done about Dulcie when he went back to New York. It had not, he saw, entered into her calculation that she should be left behind. Nor did he wish to leave her. The question was how to keep her secret well of refreshment in his active life. He could not see her or himself as members of that half world of undigested idealisms and unregulated impulses that called itself The Intellectuals. She stood for a need in his life, not the expression of a theory. But against his wish to transplant her in all her lovely and compensating isolation, there stood her beauty and his public capacity. Watching the perfection of her poses as she moved about their fire, he realized that he never would be able to hide her. He would have inevitably to account for her to his friends and possibly to his enemies. Well, she was worth accounting for! Arliss was in that mood of robust individualism which comes to a man satisfied in all his instincts, when he would have braved a great deal for Dulcie Adelaid.

And yet, as he was shortly to learn, there was very little he could save her by being brave about it. Within a day or two there drifted into their meadow the pocket hunter with his two burros and his placer pans, whose curiosity at Hawainda had been the only ripple in the smooth current of content. He came at twilight and claimed the hospitality of their evening fire. He was a bushy man with peering owl eyes that took in the obvious domesticity of their arrangements with a certain greedy unsavoriness. Dulcie was very quiet. Arliss was uncertain if she knew the man, but their visitor left them in no uncertainty as to his own knowledge.

"You're ole Tom Kennedy's gal, ain't ye?" he put it to her at last. "Thought I'd seen ye before. What ye doing with the ranch these days?"

"Rented," she told him briefly. Arliss was glad that the etiquette of the country forbade, as he understood, the personal inquisition which glittered in the pocket hunter's owlish eyes. They let the fire die out between them as the only intimation they could make of the man's unwelcomeness. Arliss was disturbed because he saw that Dulcie was, and vexed over his inability to do anything about it. Fortunately, the feed in their meadow had been cropped short by their own horses, and the next day the pocket hunter left them. When he had seen the fellow down the trail, Arliss came back and put his arms about Dulcie. She laid a hand on his mouth to forestall what might be coming.

"I haven't blamed you for anything," she said, ever so gently, but for days he had vague sensations of dissatisfaction whenever he thought of it. This was not very often, it is true, for the zest of the open life was keen in him. He savored it like a boy chewing sassafras as a harbinger of spring.

As they came over the ridge toward the house, at the end of August, they saw the dust devils dancing down the long arm of the Mesquite, beginning in a winding rush close to the ground and then spiring upward, white with scooped sand. The thin spirals moved at times down the trough of the valley before they whirled open at the top and vanished in middle air.

"It's a sign of early rains," Dulcie told him. "They will dance for a month like that, singly and by twos and threes, and then suddenly the sand storms come. Twice in a year they come, at the beginning and at the end of the rains." She showed him, as they went, how the sand drift of former years lay in the hollows, ripples marked with the direction of the prevailing winds. At Lone Tree a spring had been blotted out a year or two before by the sand.

The change in the atmosphere was easily perceptible at Hawainda. The fountain failed to rise to its customary spray, but trickled away in the track of retreating summer. Dust devils invaded the *corral de tierra* daily and doves thickened around the spring. They had to send Indian George off at once for new supplies, and clothing for Arliss. He had not come prepared for so long a stay.

"You'll need something heavier if you are to be here all winter," Dulcie warned him, looking over the list he had prepared for George. "There's considerable frost in the low places."

Was he to stay all winter? Arliss himself did not know. He was unwilling to break up so satisfactory an existence, and yet vague stirrings of recuperating powers advised him that he might presently find it monotonous. Toward the end of September, a letter reached him from his assistant in New York, intimating that, after all, lecture engagements had to be made some months in advance.

Dulcie was out with the Indian women often in these days. They were getting their winter stores of roots and seeds. Arliss read over his notes in her absence and found them good, oh, most extraordinarily good! Original, and yet subtly in line with all his old attitudes. Dulcie was at Stinking Water for the day with Catameneda, gathering a certain yellow bloom for dyes.

It was a day full of electrical prickings and atmospheric strain, that broke from time to time into hot gritty gusts. Beyond the *corral* the lower heavens had a milky tinge. Long flannelly clouds stuck midway of the ranges. About noon, Arliss, pacing restlessly in his study, saw a man coming afoot up the trail from the *corral de tierra*, stopping to take in his surroundings with what, even at that distance, was plainly an air of suspicion.

Not to invite too minute inspection, Arliss went out to meet him on the terrace, and the moment the man caught sight of him there flashed between them an indubitable spark of antagonism. At the bottom of the first terrace the stranger stopped deliberately, drew a flask from his pocket, and drank with a certain flourish, as if to say, "That's the kind of man I am." Then he shied off and began a cursory round of the premises. Arliss thought it time to interfere as the fellow displayed an intention to pass under the pergola to the patio beyond.

"What is it you want, my friend?" Arliss accosted him.

"What the hell does it matter to you what I want?"

He was a large man, younger than Arliss, and but for the ravages of drink, might have been called good looking in a crude way.

"Well, I happen to be staying here," Arliss told him, after an interval in which they took each other's measure. The fellow seemed nonplussed by that, and after a pause said less surlily, "I want to see a lady that I heard was here."

"There is no lady here." Arliss doubted his own right to say that. The man was well dressed in a careless fashion; no common prospector, it was evident. But if he had any real claim on Dulcie Adelaid he turned off without pressing it.

About a quarter of an hour later Arliss caught the man entering the patio by way of the garden.

"Now, see here," said Arliss, "this is a private residence and you have been told to keep out."

"Who's livin' here?"

"I am, and I'll give you just two minutes to clear out."

The man muttered angrily to himself. He had evidently had another pull at his flask and was beginning to be befuddled.

"Look here, ol' sport," he began thickly, "I wanna see the lady. I got business with her."

"There is no lady."

"Whur'z she? Whur'z Dulcie?" Arliss turned sick. Whatever it meant, he must get rid of this creature before it used that name again.

"Gone," he said, "gone away. I don't know when she'll be back." He hoped that would be enough. The man stood blinking and balancing.

"Gotta see Dulshie, 'portan bizzness," he fumbled for his flask, evidently with the intention of clearing up the confusion of his mind. "Have a drink," he offered sociably, and as Arliss curtly refused, "better have a drink. Had a long walk this morning. Walked all way from Cottonwood shee Dulshie." He brightened after a long pull, and asked almost sharply, "Where did you say she'd gone?"

In a flash of inspiration Arliss answered. "Gone to Lone Tree." If the fellow went there to look for her, it would give Dulcie time to be prepared before meeting him. Lone Tree was easily a day's walk away and in exactly the opposite direction from Stinking Water where the women had gone. After a few more aimless maunderings, it was the trail to Lone Tree the stranger took. Arliss followed him until he made sure that the drink-bemused mind had absorbed the impression he had meant to give.

But the incident had proved extraordinarily disconcerting. So much so that he had not got it in any sort of shape to digest by the time Dulcie came home. She came late, tired and blowsed by the wind which, from the hour of sunset, could be heard thrashing about the hills like a fretful beast. Because of her fatigue and his own nervous reaction to the weather, and the distaste he felt for the whole business, Arliss put off speaking until the last possible moment.

It was not necessary to ask if she knew who the stranger might have been; it was only too evident that she knew, and that she was extraordinarily and pitiably disturbed by his account of the visitor of the afternoon. Strangely, she was disturbed on Arliss's account. She came up to him and put her hands on him as she had done after the incident of the rattlesnake, as if to assure herself he had suffered no harm, and took her hands away again to hide their trembling.

"You're not—he didn't—he didn't do anything—threaten anything to you?"

"I have already told you that he had no idea who I am."

"Yes, I forgot." She was making desperate efforts to beat down her alarm. "Did he say anything about coming back?"

"I suppose he may come back, when he finds you are not at Lone Tree."

"Lone Tree! You sent him to Lone Tree!" So fixed had her mind been on the subject of her alarm that she had not taken this in. "What time was it? Did you notice whether he had any canteen? Did he fill it here? Did you—but of course you wouldn't have fed him?"

"Naturally," Arliss felt himself arraigned, "you don't ordinarily practice forcible feeding on chance visitors. He had a canteen and he may have filled it, but I don't think your friend cared for water. He preferred what he had in the bottle." Then, feeling that he had been unnecessarily unkind, he went over to her. "What is it about this man that so distresses you?" She put him off, moving uncertainly to and fro in the guttering candlelight.

"I don't know what to do. I don't know . . . you sent him to Lone Tree. Drunk! And a sandstorm coming. And there hasn't been any water at Lone Tree for two years!"

TOWARD morning, Arliss woke with a smothered sense that instinctively associated itself with the incidents of the night before. The dusk of dawn and the taste of dust in the air merged into a befogged and irritable frame of mind in which the instinct of kindness struggled with the conviction that Dulcie's anxiety covered something more personal than it admitted. Withal, a great sense of practical helplessness flooded back as he struggled up in bed to make out Dulcie standing in the doorway, fully dressed.

"The wind is moving up Mesquite," she told him. "Even if George got back to Cottonwood last night, he'll not think of leaving. I'm going myself to Lone Tree—"

"I'll be ready in a moment—"

"No—no, it isn't necessary." But already he had begun to dress, and presently he joined her in the kitchen where Catameneda was serving a hasty meal.

"I wish you would believe me when I say it isn't necessary for you to go," she said again, but he went on doggedly with his preparation.

"If it hadn't been for his drinking," she apologized, "it wouldn't be necessary for anybody to go. But you see, in this storm it's so easy to lose the way—and no water." Arliss saw that she was trying to erase the impression of extreme anxiety of the night before, and again the occasion seemed flavored with the bitter taste of dust that filled the air. Without a word he shouldered the canteens that Catameneda filled for him and permitted her to tie his hat down with a handkerchief. It made him feel ridiculous, but having transgressed the custom of the country in sending a drunken and disagreeable stranger to a stopped water hole, he felt he must not object to anything the two women proposed for him.

They went out by the trail that led from the bottom of the orchard, drowned in the deep blue of the desert dawning. The air lay heavy along the hills; now and then it tugged violently as at unseen bonds. Dust devils had invaded the *corral de tierra* and danced there in solemn convocation. Veiling the opposite wall of Mesquite Valley, a yellow fog rose up, traveling far into the middle sky. They had traveled for half an hour before Arliss realized that this fog was the loose surface of the desert moving on the wind.

As they rounded the hills toward Mesquite their breath was choked with dust. Dulcie led, and not until the trail dipped down into the flying yellow murk did any word pass between them.

She turned back a moment then to catch her breath as the first push of wind struck them, and as he put out his arm to steady her she looked up, instantly grateful for the smallest token of renewed interest.

"You know, it isn't in the least necessary for you to come."

"As if I should let you go alone! Besides, I sent him."

"Oh, my dear, if I said anything to blame you for that! How could you know?" She put her hands up to his shoulders in a way she had, and then nervously took them down again as if conscious of a liberty. "Promise me that whatever happens, you won't blame yourself for anything."

But he was, in fact, blaming her for everything. It had been stupid of him not to remember that there was no water at Lone Tree, but his impulse had been protective. How could he have sent an angry and drunken man to meet Dulcie Adelaid in the hills? It was no part of his business that the man had been too drunk to look after himself properly. That was the way Arliss phrased the situation to himself; but in reality the core of his dissatisfaction was the fear so peculiar to men that women never quite do justice to it, the fear of raw human reality. Convinced that the man he had sent waterless along the Lone Tree trail had some still unconfessed relation to Dulcie Adelaid, he shrunk from the sort of expression of human reality which men call "a scene."

If he kept himself from an exhibition of his fear, it was only because of a counterfear lest by any act of his he should let down the bars to the encroachment of unpleasantness. So he continued to hold her, wordless, until they were caught in the sand-laden smother of the wind. It came against them with a mighty push that veered suddenly and left them toppling over their own opposition. The sand bit into their faces, and now and then it lifted itself bodily from the ground and swept blindingly between them and their own track; their nostrils clogged with dust. Huge, dim shapes of tumbleweeds went past them in the murk like the flight of images in a disordered brain. The friction of infinite particle upon particle generated an electric tension that was all but intolerable. With it all went a slow chill that penetrated to the marrow.

All this time, at the very center of its tumultuous privacy, a part of Arliss's mind was engaged with the problem of Dulcie Adelaid. He forgot at times that she was there a few yards before him, feeling out the trail with a fine instinct that persisted in the midst of the wind and murk. The only thing that was present with him was the impress of her personality, pricked into him by the intimacy of the three months past. He had accepted her as the perfect expression of the place and occasion. He had told himself the man's fairy tale in which loving exists for its own sake from moment to moment, equally detached from its source in experience and from all its consequences; clapped in and out by desire, like those tables spread by the Genii in *Arabian Nights*.

Unskilled as most men are in relating women to their past, Arliss began in the intervals of intolerable smother to feel out her character by the impressions she had made on him, and like most men, mistook depth for duplicity. He told himself that he had always known her, not the girl she seemed, but a woman, ripened by experience. For all her reticencies there had been understanding in her warmth, knowledge in her surrender. And then the recollection of that warmth and that surrender would snatch him almost bodily out of the storm, so that only his feet stumbling in the trail recalled him.

Once Dulcie turned back to him to ask for a drink from the canteen, and the sight of her face, blue and pinched, waked him to the normal male protectiveness. He would have put himself between her and the wind, but she protested.

"You would lose the trail before you went ten steps. We've been out of it two or three times already, but I know where it ought to be. And there might be traces any minute."

They had been out for four hours and the wind increased its steady fury. If it had not been for the dips and windings of the trail that took them occasionally out of the direct path of the storm, they could not have endured against it. At the end of another hour Dulcie crept back to him. She could not spare the breath to speak, but led him by the hand through a dyke of the black rock that seamed the country, to a shallow overhung depression that might have been the lair of a fox or coyote.

"We must eat and rest," she told him. "I have a feeling, though we are still in the Lone Tree trail, that we have lost him." Often before in their outings it had happened that, all visible signs of the trail failing, she had recovered it after an interval of silence by the use of that fine instinct for direction which she had assured him was the birthright of the Indian and the outlier.

Sometimes, on such occasions, she would come back and rest upon his bosom and, as if electrified by that contact, go forward again with that light sureness which was her abiding charm. But though she must have been needing the restoring contact sorely, today she made no move to claim it, and her abnegation touched him more than any direct appeal could have done. When he had searched out a hole under the black rock and built, with the fox's litter, a little fire to warm their coffee, he reached out and drew her against his shoulder. Warmed by that nearness he made his own confession.

"I didn't know," he said, "I couldn't know when I sent him off, what this was like. I only thought how it might annoy you if you met him in the hills, and Lone Tree was the only place I could think of where you couldn't possibly be. You must believe that I never dreamed that he could come to harm."

"I know, my dear, of course I know."

"You've made the desert seem so safe to me. . . ."

"Oh, my dear, you made the *world* seem so safe. . . . It is my fault. . . . You made everything seem so *right*. . . . I couldn't imagine how anything could touch us. . . ." They murmured comfort to each other in the hollow of the storm.

The push of the wind grew steadier, though not less, while they ate and drank, and their courage steadied to meet it.

"I think he must have left the trail somewhere here," Dulcie was confident. "I can't feel him any more, and it would have been the sensible thing to do. The wind would have begun to blow by the time he reached here last night."

"If he has found something like this," Arliss began, but he saw how the sand dripped from the folds of their clothing and realized that a drunken man lying down in that terrible smother might never get up again.

"I must go back a little way," Dulcie insisted. After a quarter of an hour of beating about, half blind and numb, they picked up a whiskey flask lying unshattered on the sand. Dulcie turned the mouth of the flask to her palm and a faint ring of moisture appeared.

"He was off the trail here—" she spoke slowly, translating the slight intimations of her outdoor sense. "I think he must have decided to turn back—or—he must have gone to Dieman's. That would be it." Dieman's, she explained, was a prospector's shack at the lower end of Lone Tree cañon where it opened into Mesquite. There had been a little mine there, and Dieman had carried water in barrels from Lone Tree.

"Dieman had to leave when the spring dried. If it hadn't been for the drink, he would have remembered that." Again with her unconscious betrayal of intimacy with the idiosyncrasies of the man they followed, Arliss felt the prickle of jealous suspicion. They moved on, fumbling, for a while, and discovered a fresh break in a creosote bush, and footprints on its lee side not yet filled with the shifting sand.

Up to this time they had traveled with the wind or across it. Now they faced it down the wash of Lone Tree, their eyes and lungs filled with it intolerably. They made their way by Dulcie's knowledge of the location of the prospector's cabin, for such trail as there had been was completely overblown. A dozen times they were driven back staggering and strangled. A dozen times Arliss begged, "Give up, give up! The man is dead or safe by this time." But she struggled free of his detaining hand and faced toward Dieman's. He caught her at last in the lee of a mesquite mound where they half lay, squaring their arms about their heads to make a breathing space, and Arliss held her firmly.

"It is on my head," he shouted at her ear. "Don't make me responsible for your death also."

"I must find him, I must . . . ," she struggled feebly. "I must . . . you don't understand."

"Make me . . . make me understand. What is this man that you must risk your life for him? What is he . . . to you?"

"My husband."

« E I G H T »

IT was after about a quarter of an hour of blind groping that a sudden veering of the wind showed them the square of Dieman's cabin a hundred yards or so below them. Almost at the door they stumbled on a man's body lying face down upon his arm.

About sunset the wind dropped perceptibly. Fine sand still sifted through the cracks of Dieman's cabin and dimmed the light of one poor candle end which they had found. Arliss had broken up some loose boards and packing cases and made a fire in the cracked stove. Dulcie Adelaid's husband lay in the bare bunk, a thin ooze of blood upon his lips, which Dulcie Adelaid wiped away as it rose.

Nothing but the barest commonplaces had passed between her and Arliss since she had claimed the man in the bunk for hers. Everything that could be done under the circumstances had been done. Water had been trickled down his relaxed throat, and hot stones were at his feet. With the same unobtrusive deftness with which she had spread that first meal for him at the forsaken way station, Dulcie contrived a supper of the food they had brought.

"You must rest now," she urged him. "The wind will rise toward midnight, but by morning it will go down for a while, if not entirely. You must get back to the Lone Tree trail in time to meet Catameneda. I told her to come on after us with water and food." Arliss was touched by her concern for him.

"It is you who must rest." He turned up the rude table to break the gusts that ripped between the warped, unbattened boards, and folded his coat for a pillow. "Lie down," he said peremptorily, holding her cloak to spread over her.

Too sensible of the situation to protest, she dropped down in front of the reddening stove. At the unexpected kindness of his stooping to tuck her in, tears sprang suddenly to her eyes.

"I must tell you," she said, "let me tell you." Though he shrank from the relation, Arliss thought it might as well be then as any time.

He blew out the shrinking candle end and opened the door of the stove. It was in his mind that it would be easier to sit in the dark with a dying man than with the dead. His own private conviction that the labored breathing of Dulcie's husband might stop at any moment took something from the sordidness of the occasion. Dulcie pulled herself up sitting as he dropped down beside her in the shelter of the table.

"I hadn't seen him for two years and a half," Dulcie began. I hadn't lived with him since the first year. Only once when he— he forced me. Then I went away." She spoke quietly with long pauses in which the cabin could be felt quivering in the steady push of the wind like a reed in a freshet.

"He was my father's foreman on the ranch. He was there when I came back from the convent school, and from the very first he wanted me. My father wanted me to have him. He thought I would be safer married. And there wasn't anybody else. Only Mexicans and Indians. How was I to know about men? I didn't know—anything.

"He took me to San Francisco for our wedding journey, and right away at the hotel when I saw him among other men it began to seem dreadful that he should have me. I saw men and women there who were like my mother, and I knew they were my kind. I wanted to go with them the way a quail does with the flock in the spring. It seemed a monstrous, made-up thing that I should have to go with *him* . . . made-up. . . .

"I don't know if men ever understand what marriage is to a girl . . . and with the wrong man. . . ." She recovered herself with difficulty. "He wasn't unkind to me. Not then. He cared very much in his way." She spread her hands to the blaze as though the very memory of that way chilled her; the charm of her beauty and simplicity began to come out for Arliss again. He was certain now that there would be no "scene." The condition of the man in the bunk was so plainly due to excessive drinking that Arliss no longer suffered a sense of guilt in that connection. Dulcie Adelaid's husband would probably die in the night, to the great release of Dulcie Adelaid. She spoke of him as impersonally as if he were dead already.

"I didn't understand just at first what his way meant. Not until that summer I went up in the mountains with him to look for mavericks, and in the evening the mountain sheep came past. I called him just as I did you. He carried a revolver always of course, but I didn't think—I couldn't—but he shot them! From behind my skirts. And he laughed. The way one laughs at a child. It was always like that; what I thought, what I felt; whether I cried, or was angry, it was a trick to him and—an invitation. I was never *real* to him.

"I suppose," said Dulcie, struggling with a world-old bewilderment of women, "that my being pretty had something to do with it. He never seemed to know anything about me except what I made him feel. I could keep him off from me by *not* making him feel, by not laughing or crying or struggling with him." She lost herself in that puzzle of the self-centered passion of men, so that for the moment she seemed to have forgotten both the man beside her and the one who lay dying in the bunk. "That's how," she explained almost to herself, "that I knew it was right for me to have you. I could make you feel things that were not about me. I could make you feel stronger and clearer about things that had nothing to do with me. I thought it was right for *you* to have me, because you could do things *with* me that you couldn't do without. But I couldn't feel, in spite of being married, that it was right for *him* to have me just—just for his pleasure. I felt—exploited," she found the word finally. "And before I met you, I knew that you didn't believe in the exploitation of women."

She was silent for so long that Arliss rose to replenish the fire and took a restless turn up and down the narrow cabin. He had the average man's vague distaste for the analysis of personal relations. But he felt that he ought to say something. He came and leaned on the table looking down on her.

"You don't need to tell me all this if it pains you."

"Oh, no," she seemed surprised. "It is only that I wouldn't have pained *you*. That's why I didn't tell you before. I meant to, that day at the reservoir. But after you said what you did—about values not being established by what people have done—it didn't seem necessary. All these things seemed to me like a cruel and stupid accident that had happened to me in the past, and I didn't want you to be troubled by hearing about it. It's the way I'd have felt about you if I had known that you had—an accident like that." He was so touched by her magnanimity that he took her hand as he sat down beside her again. He began to feel certain that whatever the implications of their situation, she would somehow get them out of it. It was pitiful and endearing to think of her eluding the other man's coarse desire by that very subtlety of aloofness which was to Arliss her chief charm. It went so well with his idea of her as a creature of the desert. He had the same sort of sympathy he might have had for a young quail, hiding itself timidly in the sand at his feet.

"There isn't much more," she said. "I kept him off as well as I could, and then my father had an accident that took him to the hospital in Los Angeles. I went with him, and when he died there, I never went back. I had an excuse. One that other people would have called an excuse, I mean. There was an Indian girl at the ranch—" She threw it off with a gesture.

"I didn't get a divorce because it seemed like admitting what I wasn't willing to admit, that there was any real tie between us; that I'd ever been really married to him. Do you think it was a mistake?"

"I think most people would have considered it so."

"Yes. Yes, I suppose I must go through with it." She turned toward him with grave unexpected tenderness.

"How wonderful it is that all the things you have said and done should be just the things we need now. . . .

"Do you remember that time you came down from Ubehebe, you lit fires along the trail to let me know that you were coming. It's as if you had been lighting fires for us all these years. I don't suppose it turns out like that often with people—or does it, perhaps, if we live sincerely. I shan't be afraid, with all the flares you've made." She did not go to him, but Arliss understood that her purpose was to reassure him.

She smiled up at him with that delicate glowing shyness which was her imperishable charm. "How wonderful you are . . . wonderful."

Arliss felt that his wonderfulness, if it existed at all, lay in the success with which he concealed the uneasiness which was stirred up by her inclusion of him in the situation. He felt that he could hardly be considered "in" when so much of the situation had been concealed from him. But he had sense enough to realize that it was only by leaving the situation wholly in her hands that he could maintain his logical detachment.

He was even aware of vague movements of sympathy toward the man in the bunk, as finding himself somehow in the same case, though he did not follow the impulse back to its source in the common clouding of the male intelligence about women by the impact of their beauty on the sense. The most that he was conscious of during the hours in which Dulcie, under his persuasion, slept, was a sense of being intrigued, of being betrayed by yielding to what had seemed so natural as to be, by its very naturalness, proved right.

As the man in the bunk dropped into a deeper torpor that seemed less likely than ever to yield him back, and as the storm, after rising to a sharper fury at the turn of midnight, dropped, too, towards the dawn, Arliss's uneasiness gradually left him. More and more with the lessening of the nervous tension of the storm, he relaxed into that formless altruism, the key in which so much of his life was set, that Dulcie Adelaid knew so well how to arouse in him. He waked from four or five hours of rest, that she woke herself to impose upon him, with the renewed sense of ethical well-being, through the consciousness of having already behaved extremely well to Dulcie's besotted husband.

The sky was still deeply blue and the air heavy with dust when he set out to intercept Catameneda at the Lone Tree trail. Now and then the wind gasped convulsively like a dying creature, and the surface of sand was still arustle as it slipped back from stick and stone, like the ebb of storm-blown water.

Dulcie went half a mile with him to make sure that he had struck the trail, nearly indistinguishable since the storm. As it turned out he was glad of that, for rid of the presence of the man in the bunk, she could kiss him good-bye. And since it was the last he was to see of her in the wilderness, Arliss was glad afterwards to recall that he turned as he came to the lift of the trail and waved his hand to her.

Catameneda met him about mid-morning, turning off toward Dieman's under his direction; and from Hawainda, where he arrived late that evening, he sent Indian George back with the buckboard and team.

Then for two days he waited in the empty house unable to think either of the past or the future. There were letters in the mail that George had brought, calling him to New York as nothing else had done those months past, but his scruples about leaving

Dulcie Adelaid with a drunk and possibly dying man on her hands kept him from responding. And the sand that choked the fountain and tattered the leaves of the artichoke lay as thickly in his mind over the pleasant by-paths of the summer past. So he lived from hour to hour, watching the Lone Tree trail from the bottom of the orchard for two days, which is as long as a man can manage without going forward or back. At the end of that time a strange Indian brought him a note from Dulcie, saying that as her husband—whose name it struck him oddly he had not heard—seemed so much worse, she was going on with him to Barstow where there was a doctor. Arliss's mind, released from its tension, leaped forward with a bound.

THOSE of his followers who were privileged to hear Grant Arliss on his first platform appearance after his return from the West never forgot it. It was like hearing a musician whose technique has always been admitted to be faultless, but lacking in temperament, and then after an interval hearing him burst suddenly into full power. Younger men who had gathered around him chiefly out of their own desperate hope for *something,* some way out of their own political sterility, men who had felt that Arliss *could* produce the materials of fire, and had yet remained doubtful if he *would,* found themselves dazzled into confidence. Dazzled and yet warmed. There was a blaze, a sensible heat, clear and without smoke.

That was the first reaction. And then a question, a faint toppling sensation as when a door against which you have thrown your weight, gives suddenly. To think that after all your struggle the thing should prove so simple. Dazzlingly simple. There wasn't, it seemed to be, any program; there was to be a movement, an unfolding of a scroll of political intention whereon the party was to read as it ran the precise measures by which a particular emergency was to be met. No program and no precedent. The one thing was as stultifying as the other, left no room for the operation of that political instinct, that inner sense of the folk for its own right way, which it had been the original intention of democracy to uncover. The new party was to return to this primary concept of democracy as a force rather than a program of performance. It was to go forward under its own power, its own innate laws. That was to be the program, the logical appearance of the law of "democracy in action"; you couldn't, for instance, imagine that at any time any measure of exploitation of one class by another class could be allowed by the operation of true democracy. Advocacy of the child labor bill would be inevitable and natural, labor provisions which had their source in the natural exigencies of labor. One by one he named measures and tendencies which came within a liberal interpretation of the open road of political progression. But no move of the party was ever to commit the party, in advance, to another move.

Those of Arliss's following who found themselves frankly blinded by this shining simplicity were reassured by the man himself. They found him greatly improved by his Western holiday. Filled out; bodily and, well, personally. If this prospectus of the future seemed a trifle sketchy, there was no doubt that the man himself had gained in poise and sureness. No doubt, the inner circle of his adherents assured themselves, Grant Arliss had his feet on the ground. And for the touch-and-go quality of his political astuteness, look at the way he had drawn old Henry Rittenhouse into his following.

Arliss's first appearance on his return had been before a small, selected audience. The second had been in Carnegie Hall, jammed to the ceiling. And at the end of the address the eager and congratulatory group around the speaker had parted suddenly to let in Alida Rittenhouse. They knew who she was; knew that old Henry trusted her judgment to the extent of taking it, in respect to younger figures rising on the political scene, figures not quite of his generation but of continuing force. Sharp, almost breathless silence widened around Arliss as she came forward holding out her hand, simply gracious and smiling.

"I've a message for you, Mr. Arliss, from my father. It wasn't possible for him to get away, but he hoped you'd come to see him." There was no one in the group around Arliss who did not feel certain that the giving of that message had been left wholly at the discretion of the daughter; that her giving it was the accolade of the old senator's approval. Miss Rittenhouse herself made no concealment of its being specifically pertinent. "Shall we say Thursday. To dinner then? We're staying at the Gotham."

The old senator said very little that was definite, of his own attitude or intention, so far as Arliss's declaration of political outlook was concerned. "I read your speech in the papers," he remarked when he was settling to his cigar after the meal. "It was a timely note. An exceedingly timely note. The people aren't ready to have anything shouldered on to them. But I should say they'd come along; they'll come along handsomely the way you go at them." And then he began to discourse explicitly on the moves of the game at Washington, things that could and couldn't be done. It was taken for granted that Arliss was to do them. All through the interview Alida sat close to her father's elbow with that complete acceptance of his own as well as her father's importance and of herself as a suitable background for it, which was the source in Arliss of a strange tug of homesickness. He did not, however, admit it to his consciousness as in any way connected with Dulcie Adelaid.

Already that episode was being blown over in his memory, buried as he had found the fountain in the patio on his return to it after the storm, with the clean sand of relief. The desert that gave had taken again. Nothing was left to rot and fester. He had suffered, for a day or two, as he waited for the return of Indian George and Catameneda under a devastating sense of desolation. And then had come the Indian woman with a note from Dulcie, a clean direct note with what was, to Arliss, a noble gesture of release; "I will write you," the note said, "at New York." From Barstow there had been another direct and characteristic missive saying only that she was taking her husband to a sanatorium in

southern California, but giving no address. With that letter Arliss
felt every trace of annoyance, uneasiness, and blame smooth
out, as he had seen the surface of the desert in the desert wind.
But in the presence of Alida Rittenhouse he was conscious of a
premonitory gnawing at his heart, as announces to the average
human frame the approach of mealtime. He was not as much
hungry as aware that at sometime or another he had eaten a satisfying meal, and that he would certainly eat again.

He saw much of the Rittenhouses, father and daughter, in the
next few weeks, at their Washington house, and at Thanksgiving time as house guest at Sandy Cove. And between political
conferences he discovered in himself new appreciations and re-
sponses to the accomplished domesticity of Alida, the cozy fire,
the shaded light, the choice but simple meals. Such things as
these, he told himself, were the norm, and the touchstone of reality. Something to be enjoyed, honored, defended, and forever
exempt from the acute rationalization with which all other problems, social, economic, political, were to be met.

It did not occur to him to estimate the factor of the Rittenhouse wealth in the total effect which the daughter of the Rittenhouses produced on him. All this atmosphere of peace and
creature comforts, which she had only to touch a button or give
an order to produce, seemed to proceed from her like an attri-
bute, as native, as indisseverable as the experiences that had
produced Dulcie Adelaid. The lovely certainty about Alida Rittenhouse was that the processes of her making never would be
obtruded. If he married her, and by Thanksgiving time Arliss
knew that he was looking forward to marrying her not only as an
excellent thing to do for himself but as an exquisite and informing experience, she would be a perpetual warming fire in the
presence of which he would never have any occasion to think of
the chemistry or materials of combustion.

The tradition of the next month or two of Grant Arliss's

career—it is still a tradition with power to charm and move—glowed with the color of great expectation. The number of his adherents augmented. General opinion was electrified by a new political surmise. Even the opposition judged him good-naturedly as likely to give them "a run for their money."

Then in the midst of one of his popular afternoon addresses—he was crowding them into all hours of the day now—he was aware of a delicate cobweb of distraction, of apprehension, brushed away, and obstinately returning; something that took shape at last as an incredible reality in the figure of Dulcie Adelaid. There she was in the front row of the balcony, looking down at him with raptness and delight. Between this unconvincing figure and the phrases of his speech, which, he judged from the response of his audience, proceeded with habitual success, there was an awful, widening gap of consternation into which all his energies were concentrated in the effort not to fall. He could hear his own voice rising and soaring, full of warmth and color, and at the same time could feel the effort of his intelligence to bridge across that gap in some way which would enable him somehow to pretend that it didn't exist. It wasn't true, it couldn't be possible that Dulcie Adelaid's presence there in New York could have anything to do with him.

Immediately on the close of the lecture he found himself disposing summarily of the congratulatory murmur to make a clear space for his meeting with Dulcie Adelaid. For he would have to meet her. He rushed to it in fact, as a man takes a running jump into cold water.

And then, when it happened, just outside the door, in the oblivion created by the homing rush of the crowd, he perceived suddenly that he had little to fear. He had shaken hands with her for no longer than a handshake ordinarily lasts, and yet long enough to discover that Dulcie Adelaid had no effect on him whatever.

They turned into the avenue on which lights were beginning to glow through the early dusk. The note of traffic rose around them to the high-keyed hum of home-going. A still delight exhaled like a fragrance from Dulcie Adelaid; she looked with the pleased incurious wonder of a child at the piled-up plunder of the world which glittered on them from behind the plate glass windows. She had the air of one to whom the city has come as an inheritance for the enjoyment of which all life suffices. As his eyes roved over her figure, thinner than he remembered it, her dress, correct but unseductive, and her provincial unconsciousness of herself as a figure of the scene which so intrigued her, Arliss recovered something of his poise in successive discoveries of his own immunity. With the level of his own appreciations set for him by Alida Rittenhouse, what could he fear in the wife—a gust of apprehension took him at the possible significance of her plain black garments—from the widow even, of the man he last remembered breathing drunkenly in the bunk at Dieman's. He snatched the memory of that man to him as a defense against what might be implied in the black dress and hat, which did not particularly become Dulcie Adelaid.

He was too much the special political pleader not to know that he must not begin this interview with Dulcie Adelaid against him. At the same time he was not altogether a cad. The helping hand which he had on a second saving impulse stretched out to her, dropped unnoticed, but if his coldness had set her aloof it had not disconcerted her.

On the way back to his rooms she had told him how she came, at what hotel she was staying, meager details of her journey and her search for him. She began now with the broken thread of the last occasion of their being together. She had taken her husband to Barstow and from there to Los Angeles where lately he had died. Not, she hastened to assure him, of anything that had happened to him in the sandstorm, but from drink and from the recurrence of an old trouble which, so the doctors had told her, had been the original source of his habit of drinking.

"There was nothing," she said, "for which you could blame yourself. But I was to be blamed. It was what I had done, what that man who saw us at Ubehebe told him, that set him to drinking at the last so horribly." She went on, unmindful of Arliss's thinking, his irritated sense of its not mattering in the least what had been thought; and full of Dulcie Adelaid's husband, he didn't remember that when he came to himself. "All that he remembered was that he had been looking for me and had found me. I didn't tell him anything. Not because I wanted to deceive him, but because he was too ill. Afterward, when I began to understand, I was glad I hadn't. That was one of the reasons why I never wrote—first because I didn't know how things would turn out, and then because I did know." She was talking quite simply and naturally, with full confidence in the pertinence of what she had to say. "I didn't want him to know, ever. And I had always heard people say that if there is any time when the dead *do* know it is just after—" She turned toward Arliss for the first time in her narrative, measuring his capacity to understand. "He held on to life so," she said, full of gentle sympathy for the dead. "I didn't want him to be disappointed, if—if he was still where he could feel and know about me. We—you and I—had all our lives ahead of us, and there was only that short time for him. So I went back to Sweetwater for a while, and—waited." She seemed to wait herself for confirmation. Arliss choked.

"That was sweet of you," he managed. Evidently things were going to be much more difficult than he had anticipated.

"You see," said Dulcie Adelaid, "he really cared, the way *we* cared. I suppose I had to care for someone myself before I could understand how he suffered. They told me at the ranch that he had sworn he would kill me . . . after the pocket hunter told him about us, you know." The gentle extenuation of her voice in-

cluded Arliss as well as her husband. It was as if she shook out
and folded away the garments of the dead for the last time. "I
thought I could understand that, too, about killing. . . . It would
be self-defense. When people are tortured more than they can
bear . . . if I had known what I was doing, he'd have had the
right. I'd have felt like that myself if I had been in his place. I
realized that the only thing that saved me was the recollection of
how we had always agreed together, you and I, about people not
having the right to seek their own way at the expense of other
people."

Arliss made inarticulate noises in his throat. Over and above
his personal annoyance he felt the old conviction that women were
too personal for social exigencies. He was vexed with Dulcie
Adelaid for having spoiled her case with him. But Dulcie did
now know that she was making out a case. She fumbled in her
purse and brought out a little handful of clippings.

Only half intentionally he directed their course toward his
rooms. She had obviously surrendered the management of their
hour to him, and he did not know what else to do with it. There
was something which he would have to tell her, the sooner the
better for his credit and her peace; and the male dread of the personal encounter not of his initiation guided his feet to cover.

There was no one in evidence as he let them both into the once-
pretentious hall of the made-over residence between Madison
Square and Thirteenth Street, and preceded Dulcie up the curved
stair. The room was dark with the early winter dusk, irradiated
by the reflections of the street. In the moment before he could
find the gas in the gilded chandelier of an earlier date, he felt
Dulcie's body huddled against him, her hands upon his shoulders, and the soft seeking of her face for his. With a cold sinking,
Arliss kept his arm about her formally as he guided her to a chair
and made a light. He knew now unmistakably what had brought
Dulcie Adelaid to New York.

When he dared to look at her, she had taken off her hat as if it hindered her; as if, as he had seen her so often in the desert, the more easily to assimilate herself to the part she had to play. For he saw at once that she had withdrawn herself into that curious aloofness into which he at no time had been able to follow her. She sat taking in the careless bachelor comfort of his apartment with a measuring eye, as if at the same time she took the measure of her own capacity to match with it.

As he fussed about with the curtains and the fire, Arliss had misgivings. Perhaps after all, he should have kissed her, should have made use, in view of what he had to say to her, of his easy personal ascendancy, to bias her on his side.

"I don't know how I would have gone through with it, if the papers hadn't begun to print things about you," she said. "I didn't know before how much one can suffer about another person. I thought of all the people who could see and hear you every day— touch you—people to whom it wouldn't matter in the least. . . .

"And then I found *this*," she drew out the clipping from the others, laying it against her cheek as if she sought an accustomed comfort. "What you said about the only sound politics being an expression of the reality of human experience. *Then* I had the courage to stay and let the experience do all it could for me."

As Arliss continued to pace up and down the room, she went to him with that beautiful free movement which prevailed over all her shyness. "So, that's over," she said, laying her hands with the old gesture on his breast. Arliss caught at them and at the word.

"Well over," he began, and began also to stammer.

"Isn't it wonderful about us," said Dulcie Adelaid, "that the first thing I heard you say, when I came, is the very thing I need, about the *rights* of people taking precedence over what we *feel* about them!" She quoted from his speech of the afternoon, show-ing him through her lifted face a little of that pure incandescence of the spirit that had been to him the lure of the desert and the woman. Arliss looked hastily at his watch.

"You must let me take you somewhere for dinner! How careless of me to let you go on like this. I am afraid I am always a little inconsiderate just after talking, it takes so much out of me." He had offered this as the first excuse that occurred to him and was ashamed to see how well it answered.

"You put so much of yourself into it! It is I who am careless! But not tonight; I've only got here you know. Tomorrow if it suits you." She came and put up her face to be kissed, and Arliss, too grateful for respite, did not refuse her.

THE cafe which Arliss chose for his dinner with Dulcie Adelaid was quiet without being too secluded; it had become an unconscious part of his social policy to avoid, in his relations with women, any appearance of privacy. The same instinct had led him to select, for a dinner at which there must be talk of the most private import, a place where there would be the discreet cover of music and dancing. Dulcie Adelaid was charmed with everything. She had made what he supposed was her idea of an evening toilette, but her shyness was wholly untouched by any feeling of unsuitability as she took in enjoyingly the soft lights, the sure and simple appointments. Arliss, who had begun the evening as a task calling for all his powers of personal ascendancy, had a moment of bleak wonder whether that air of being always at ease with her surroundings which had so charmed him in the desert did not proceed from a certain obtuseness which made his celebrated fineness a flimsy instrument.

It was between the roast and the salad, when after a calming interval in which her interest in his work and his political plans had come uppermost, that she said, letting her gaze wander appreciatively over the scene, bright and yet restrained, "It was beautiful of you to bring me to a place like this for the first time. We must come here often."

"We shall," he agreed, taking the plunge, "as often as possible, though I'm rather more occupied than usual just now. I'm sure you'll understand when I tell you what hasn't yet been announced, that in addition to all I have been telling you I am engaged to be married."

At the moment, Dulcie's face was turned from him, taking in the color and strangeness of the scene. Arliss dared not turn his own eyes from it, lest in the mere act of letting them fall there should slip from him something of his own grip on the situation. He saw her lovely contours stiffen as the meaning of his words reached her, and the sudden convulsive clutch of her throat as she turned back for a moment of uncertainty.

"Married?" she said. "You are engaged to be . . . married!" And not to me! were the words that hung suspended in her tone. Then slowly, as one arrested on the brink sees the abyss widening below, horror grew in her look, in her pose, in the low wordless cry which seemed squeezed from her by the pressure of certainty. She pushed back from the table a little, taking him in as the author of her pain, with wide, unbelieving eyes. Good heavens, was she really going to make a scene!

"Drink," he urged, pouring her water. "You've dropped your napkin—Waiter!" He covered her confusion with the demand for another, and once he had looked away, he could not for the life of him look back. But Dulcie Adelaid was too stricken for expression. Under the compulsion of his suggestion she made motions that might easily have been mistaken for dining.

"You mean—" Dulcie Adelaid was coming out of her stunned condition with the slow precision of intellect that was characteristic of her. "*Since* you've come back, you've . . . fallen in love with someone. Someone that you've promised to marry?"

"I'd have written you, of course," Arliss lied swiftly, "but I hadn't your address." Really, considering the way she'd left him in the dark, he couldn't allow her to think she had a grievance.

"I suppose I may know her name?"

"I can't discuss her."

It was unquestionably the traditional move, but tradition had no hold on Dulcie Adelaid. Hot anger surged up to her lovely eyes and sharpened her like a knife.

"If she is willing to take my place she shouldn't object to my taking an interest in her. Unless—" Dulcie gathered knowledge slowly through her stricken eyes. "Unless, you mean . . . she doesn't know . . ."

In justice to Arliss it must be said that he had no measure for the deeper bite of anguish which that fact held for Dulcie Adelaid. Did she really suppose a man discussed this sort of thing with the girl he expected to marry? Dulcie Adelaid had speaking eyes. As she fixed them steadily on him, Arliss felt an uneasy stir across his consciousness. She had, after all, supposed it. In some obscure way which he could not fathom, the certainty that she was not to be considered was more painful to Dulcie Adelaid than the fact that she had been supplanted. He saw by the groping movement of her hands across the tablecloth that she was sinking under successive waves of revelation that tossed her drowningly toward the pit. Man-like, the pain of her pain drove him to be sharp with her.

"Try and go on with your dinner," he said. "People are beginning to look at us."

Dulcie made a movement to brush the scene aside. Nothing mattered now but knowing what had happened to her. "You haven't, then, consulted her about this, any more than you have consulted *me*? You've just dropped me—and taken her on—and neither of us is to say a word. I'll have to think . . . I don't know what to do."

"I'm sure you'll always do what's right and fine. That's one of the things I've always felt sure about you." Arliss skimmed cautiously like a skater rounding a dangerous turn; but it was the wrong turn for Dulcie Adelaid.

"Ah, but you couldn't have, or you'd have known that I wouldn't, that I couldn't have done what I did—if I hadn't thought—if I hadn't believed—" He saw miserably what she had believed. But why *did* women go into these things as if they didn't know how they always turned out. He must get her away from here as quickly as possible.

He rose promptly as the distress of what was in her mind brought her stumbling to her feet, and tried to cover it with the business of helping her into her coat. "Wait for me outside. I've got to settle with the waiter. Try and control yourself!" he urged.

For a moment Dulcie Adelaid came to herself, taking in his anxiety and the crowded diners, most of whom were already beginning to watch them curiously. "I see," she said, "you've brought me here to shoot me behind their skirts."

There was nothing for Arliss to do but to move miserably beside her as she turned toward the street. He had heard men say that this sort of thing was always unpleasant, but he had no idea it was so unpleasant as this. He didn't, of course, think badly of the poor girl; but as for telling her in a crowded restaurant, well, he had been justified. Otherwise she *would* have made a scene.

Dulcie stumbled going across the corner of the park toward her hotel. Arliss put out his hand to her arm and felt her tremble.

"My dear, you don't know how sorry—"

"Oh," she caught at him. "You . . . *you!* That *you* should do such a thing like this! I'd *heard* of such things—men who used all the forms of honor and highmindedness to get what they all the time meant to throw away—"

"Dulcie, come be sensible." She clung to him.

"My dear, my dear . . . before I had touched you, before I had stopped the ache in my heart from doing without you, from hearing your voice, before I knew how things had been with you and what you thought and felt, to tell me *this*—"

"Dulcie, I couldn't let you go on—I had no idea—"

He was immensely sorry for her and also horribly afraid that she was going to break out crying in the street. She went on, however, until they came to the light streaming from the door of her hotel. She stepped back then a moment to compose herself.

"I want you to understand," she said, "that I don't blame you for loving somebody else, though I thought, of course, you would have—have protected me from that possibility while—while I was away." But she had already told him what had been going on with her. "If you had come to me and told me, I'd have done everything in the world to untie the knot between us—We could have untied it together. But now—I must think—we must talk." This, Arliss reflected, would never do at all.

"My dear girl," he said, "it is of no use for me to tell you how sorry I am, but don't you think it is better to let things be as they are?" She was silent a while, falling into one of those attitudes of remoteness he knew so well, detached alike from her grief and the cause of it.

"You mean," she said, "that having settled the matter for yourself, you think it is equally concluded for me?"

He was honestly surprised. "Why, how else could it be?"

She gave him a slow, wondering look. "It might have been . . ." she hesitated, "it might have been." She looked at him, keen and grave, as he had never seen her. "It might have been treated as partly *my* affair, also. And hers. I think I'll have to talk with—with the other woman."

"You will . . . you! Don't you dare! You hussy—if I catch you, disturbing—anybody—I'll know how to deal with you!" Dulcie Adelaid staggered back from the rage, the fear, the madness of vexation in his face, as from a hot blast. Dumb, hurt, and anguished unbelief stared at him from her startled eyes, burning toward a horror of convictions, and with a low animal cry of pain she turned and ran from him with the stagger of a wounded wild creature toward its lair.

ALL that night and during the two intervening days before he saw her again, Arliss told himself steadily with a dogged persistency that he had been wrong. He was wrong to have initiated the affair without an explicit understanding, wrong not to have forced a note of finality into his parting with Dulcie Adelaid by the stopped spring. It was one of the things he had drilled into himself as part of his preparation for a political career, that if he didn't get on with people, it was his fault. Politics was the business of persuading other people; and the whole art of persuasion lay in sympathy with the other fellow's point of view. That was the way he got on so well with labor; he was always sympathetic to it; where other politicians made promises, Grant Arliss sympathized, and labor made promises to him. So in the midst of intolerable anger and alarm and a conviction of being badly dealt with by fate, Arliss steadily dinged into himself that he was wrong about Dulcie Adelaid. It was his business to sympathize with her point of view—which he told himself was outrageous—and conduct his own part of the affair accordingly.

So far as he could make out her point of view, she wanted to be treated as if her interest in the situation was equal to his, as if in fact, she was still in the situation, as if, in spite of his having distinctly abandoned the situation himself, she still had some power over it. Well, he would humor her to that extent, he would listen to her, draw out the poison of her wound in talk—he would do whatever she wanted except allow her to go to Alida Rittenhouse. He would prevent that if he had to take the senator into his confidence himself. He wasn't so sure old Henry hadn't a fund of experience to draw upon. On the point of Dulcie Adelaid disturbing Alida Rittenhouse he would be firm; kind, but inexorably firm. He wished to be kind. Until now his whole life had conspired to keep him in the position of being kind. The picture of himself as the source of suffering in others filled him with a sincere misery almost as acute as the thought of his own suffering at someone else's hands. By dint of keeping it up, amid his excited imaginings of what Dulcie Adelaid might do to his career should she prove impervious to kindness, Arliss managed by the afternoon of the next day to dispatch to her a note in which he took, humbly, the tack of having blundered in an effort to be kind according to his lights, and offering himself for any time in which she felt calm enough to talk with him. To this the only answer had been that there was no answer, and as that day and another went by, he grew steadily easier in his mind. The recollection of Dulcie's poise and docility grew upon him reassuringly; it worked, with his reiterated suggestion of sympathy and kindness, like a charm.

So when he discovered her waiting for him in the street a block or two from his rooms, on the evening of the third day, he was so far recovered in equanimity that he was able to speak very kindly to her.

He was sincerely stricken in his susceptibilities, when as they passed under the flare of the street lamp, he saw what had gone on in her; the wreck and damage of illimitable despair. If he had seen her face first and not her firm young figure and her free walk, he would not have known her. To his credit, he was incredibly touched by her appearance even before he was relieved by her first word.

"I came to say good-bye," she told him tonelessly, "I'm going back to Sweetwater tonight. . . . I'd like to go up to your room for a little while." There was a great weariness in her voice, and the appeal of finished sorrow in her face. Arliss put out his hand to hers and drew it through his arm. The street was very quiet; the purples of winter twilight contended in the shadows with the yellows of the electric lamps. The pavement echoed frostily to the feet of infrequent passersby. They walked the length of the block before Arliss spoke. "I've been wondering what had become of you." He meant her to know that he meant to be kind.

"Oh, I've been thinking—and talking to your friends. Oh, not telling them things—" as his instant uneasiness communicated itself along his arm, "asking things. Things about your work the newspapers couldn't tell me. I have been trying to find out if your ideas are something meant to be lived, or just . . . talk."

"I am afraid you always had too high an opinion of me, Dulcie." Poor girl, he must allow her a little bitterness.

"Yes," she admitted drearily, "I guess I was just—innocent. I thought they were things to be lived by, the things you said. They were—they are—the sort of things I live by myself. You understand that, don't you?"

"As far as I can understand how social principles *can* be personal—I'm sure you never did anything but what you thought was right, my dear."

"Yes," she said, again. "But you see, I thought it was just the point you made that there wasn't to be any difference between what was social and what was personal, not any difference in rightness." She turned her fine eyes upon him, dark now with despair. "I don't think so now," she said.

"My dear, my dear," he murmured. What other answer could he make? This at any rate seemed to serve, for she fell silent beside him.

The hall had not been lit when he let her in with his latchkey, and by the light from the street he let in with her, she passed on ahead of him up the dark turn of the stair. Arliss halted a moment as his habit was, to turn over the letters laid on the newel; his landlady, hearing him, came out to hold a wax lighter to the gas. She had the greatest respect for Mr. Arliss as a prompt-paying lodger and a pleasant-spoken gentleman, and that was how it was she was able to testify when it was required of her, that he had gone to his rooms a little past six, alone, and that no one after that had gone up to him.

"Don't make a light," Dulcie had said to him, as he let her into his room, faintly illuminated from the street, "I shall only be a moment." She moved over to the window as Arliss removed his hat and coat, turning as she heard him come toward her.

She put her hands up to his shoulders the old way; he felt her tremble, and he put his arm about her reassuringly, meaning to be kind.

"I wanted to see you," she began, "I wanted to make sure. To make sure . . . if it was ever real . . . if there was ever *anything* real at all."

"Dulcie, I'm sorry this has turned out badly for you. I never meant—"

"No you never meant—*anything*. You just—*felt*." He moved uneasily and she quieted. "So I wasn't real to you, ever," she spoke despairingly, almost to herself. "I was just used—exploited—in the eternal war—the war between men and women."

"I hoped, Dulcie, we could part in kindness."

"Yes. I don't come to quarrel. My train leaves in an hour. If it is to be good-bye—"

"Good-bye—" He felt her arms go about him and a sudden surprising pain in his side like a thorn. "Dulcie!" He had time to say her name again, in a great terror of blackness, before she eased him quietly to the floor.

Dying thus, at the flood tide of his career, Grant Arliss had the public advantage of being remembered as martyr to the cause of justice and true democracy to which he had dedicated the life so lost. For when the weapon which had been found thrust deep into his heart had been passed upon by the savants of the police, it was shown to have been the sort that could only have been used by the professional gangster who had made himself the tool of the political ring, whose peace and profits Arliss had so successfully disturbed, and from whom he was known to be the recipient of anonymous threats. There was nothing known of Arliss or his life which could connect the weapon, "a thorn-shaped dagger of foreign workmanship, the ivory handle mended with bone," with the figure of a young woman who at the moment this decision was being arrived at was staring blindly at the fleeting of Western landscape past the windows of the Overland Flier, her face slowly setting into the torpor of relief after great shock and pain.

WHEN Dulcie Adelaid sticks her dagger, her cactus thorn, into Grant Arliss's side, her action reflects Mary Austin's belief that there was no "difference between what was social and what was personal" (95).[1] When she wrote the last sentence of the novella, she, like Dulcie Adelaid, must have settled back with a feeling of relief, having finished off the final version of a character she had been creating, in various guises, for years: the radical male whose behavior falls short of his social vision, who fails to recognize what feminists of all generations have insisted upon, that the personal *is* political.

Austin had known such men—and had an affair with one of them—during a decade of turbulent New York life, when she was caught up in most of the radical political movements of her day: friendly with many leading activists and intellectuals, she worked for suffrage, for labor reform, for birth control, for communal kitchens to free women workers during World War I.[2] In a novel about her New York years, *No. 26 Jayne Street*, which she called a "war novel from the American woman's point of view," Austin had explored the "progressive" male's unwillingness to rethink his relations to and attitudes about women; the novel, she said, "aimed to uncover the sleazy quality of current radicalism, the ways in which the personal expression of radicals contradicted and reversed the political expression" (*Earth Horizon*, 337).[3] Frustrated by her own unhappy marriage, Austin believed, like Dulcie Adelaid, that marriage was "made up," a social construct, and much of her work considers how to reshape the relationships between women and men. Like many other feminists, she felt particularly disillusioned when male reformers did not share her commitment to restructuring the private life.

Austin eventually tired of New York and its "Intellectuals," beckoned West once again by desert trails and solitude and her interest in southwestern cultures. She wanted to conclude her life living in and writing about the desert. But she was not yet done with the New York radicals; she wanted to explore whether the West's "naked spaces" would enlarge one urban reformer's social vision. In *Cactus Thorn* she brings together characters who represent the two spheres of her adult experience: her years in New York as a political activist and her years as a desert wanderer seeking escape from her marriage and developing her vision and her style. Like the artistic desert mystics of Austin's earliest stories, characters whose vision is intimately tied to that landscape she believed uncramped the soul, Dulcie Adelaid has "the mark of the land" upon her, and though Grant Arliss can use her, as he uses the desert, "to be filled again, to be warmed and quickened" (17), he can never "fathom" her.[4] He indulges his needs at her expense, but he does not learn from her what she, like Austin, learned from the desert: how to "live sincerely" (74).

Dulcie Adelaid's life reflects Austin's spiritual engagement with the desert. Like the horned toad that blends organically into the "tawny earth," Dulcie is in complete harmony with the land she describes as "like a woman," an image Austin had developed in "The Land."[5] Like Austin, she developed her vision—outward and inward—through patient observation of apparently empty land and her speech in response to the "open country" and its "vastness" (9). Like Austin, she learned the meaning of creativity—to be "sensitive to the spirit of existence"—by watching Native American women go through the everyday motions of living (*Earth Horizon*, 362).[6] A seeker, she follows the desert footsteps of another Austin character, the Walking Woman, who "walked off all sense of society-made values, and, knowing the best when the best came to her, was able to take it" ("The Walking Woman," 97).[7]

Dulcie Adelaid associates the desert with her rebellion from "society-made values": "'That's the best thing you get out of the desert,'" she says. "'It teaches you never to make anything up'" (9–10). She rejects a marriage she finds unnatural, "made-up." Pressured by her mother, in 1891 Austin had married "the wrong man," Wallace Austin, an intelligent but unreliable desert drifter, who, as she put it, "never looked with me at any single thing" (*Earth Horizon*, 243). Lonely and isolated, she had hoped for intellectual companionship; ignorant about her own sexuality, she had assumed that passion would follow marriage vows. Her response to her marriage is neatly summed in the odd title to a story about a woman whose creative energies are stifled by her expectation that marriage will provide her with emotional and intellectual fulfillment: "Frustrate."[8] Dulcie's challenge to marriage echoes Austin's belief that the redefinition of sexual roles in marriage belonged at the heart of any new social theory. To Arliss's way of thinking, she had the annoying feminine tendency of "'lead[ing] the subject back to sex,' when it so clearly had to do only with economics" (37).

Throughout *Cactus Thorn* Austin mocks Arliss's failure to see the personal implications of his "economic" ideas. In a novel in which women and land are symbolically united, the following passage is especially ironic:

> Arliss found in her description [of mining] his favorite indignation. That, he protested, was how men went about the earth, snatching and rending, and even as they tore at the hills for a handful of gain, they despoiled and exploited one another. Once he was launched on the social protest he slipped easily into the born politician's facility of denunciation, and quoted freely from himself. (36)

Arliss cannot recognize that the male need to possess and conquer land is echoed by the desire to feel a "pulse of power" over
women. With her holistic philosophy about the integration of
one's actions with one's beliefs, Dulcie Adelaid interprets such
political statements as evidence that Arliss opposes the "exploitation of women" (73). But he readily borrows the terms of capitalism when he thinks of women. He feels a sense of "proprietorship" over Dulcie, and he ultimately rejects her because he holds
the traditional view that she "belongs" to another man and because his metaphor for a wife, "a fenced and valued possession,"
cannot encompass her (51). In fact, questions about women and
marriage are not central to Arliss's thinking: he recognizes that
"his freedom from any disposition to make over the marital relations of society had been an important item of his success in suggesting that it could be made over politically" (15). Austin
believed, of course, that one could not be made over without the
other, and she exposes how Arliss's "vague distaste for the analysis of personal relations" impedes his understanding (73).

Arliss lives his life by a series of fictions. Although he con-
gratulates himself on his "moral impeccability" and scorns his
fellow radicals who freely discuss sex, he pursues Dulcie Adelaid, perhaps inspired by an engineer who seems to step from the
pages of Annette Kolodny's *Lay of the Land*, describing the "man-
size job to conquer" the "round-bosomed hills and the cradling
dip of the land" (22).[9] As Austin suggests through repeated fire
imagery, Arliss's attraction to her is passionate and sexual. Yet he
seeks a sexual relationship out of a need for the energy and inspiration which accompany passion, not out of any real interest
in Dulcie herself: "If only he could find a woman who could be
counted on to kindle a flame and keep it going, he might, at that
glow, warm the slowly chilling reaches of his intellect and his
ambition" (12). Arliss is a parasite. He sees only the mystery and
romance of the desert and of Dulcie; he makes no real attempts to
understand either.

Austin lampooned Arliss's kind of love in another novel, *Love and the Soul-Maker:*

> If you will talk very directly with almost any free lover, you will find that what he really expects of the free alliance is a state of things in which you are to be noble enough to let him go, should his happiness demand it, but he is not required to be noble enough to stay, should your welfare be in question.[10]

At the first "encroachment of unpleasantness," Arliss falls back upon "the man's fairy tale in which loving exists for its own sake from moment to moment," detached "from all its consequences" (65). By the end of the novel, Arliss hides behind his self-justifications, as Dulcie Adelaid's husband hid behind her skirts. In drawing this analogy between them, Austin suggests how both men threaten life, and thus Arliss presents an implicit threat to Dulcie and to her values: "an artist . . . is sensitive to the spirit of existence. Living things . . . symbolize this sense of existence" (*Earth Horizon*, 362).

Arliss's fatal flaw, as a man and as a politician, is his unconscious hypocrisy, his shortsighted self-knowledge, a flaw Austin brilliantly reveals by presenting the story through his restricted consciousness and giving us insight into what he fails to see. Caught up in romantic visions of the desert and of Dulcie, he does not recognize, for instance, their danger, though Austin drops liberal hints: the thorn hidden beneath the beautiful flower; the lure of mirages and threat of a blinding sandstorm; the implications of the mother's dagger, given for protection against men who cannot control their desire; the rattlesnake that threatens the intimacy displayed as Arliss watches Dulcie Adelaid return her knife to its sheath on her garter; the conversations about what Arliss considers her "quaint philosophy" that morality is relative, defined by personal integrity and consistency, and that those who "go against their Medicine, as the Indians say," will ultimately be punished. When Arliss betrays Dulcie's vision of him, as someone who "'spread[s] justice and honesty into business and trade and society,'" he earns his end (54).

By the conclusion of *Cactus Thorn*, set in a New York where political convolutions and alliances echo the city's urban mazes and contrast the desert's *open* space, Austin so entraps her readers in Arliss's consciousness, with its condescending assessments of Dulcie Adelaid and its squirming self-justifications, that many readers no doubt welcome his death in order to be free of him. Some readers will question whether Arliss deserved to die; like Susan Glaspell's feminist classic "A Jury of Her Peers" (1917), *Cactus Thorn* is disturbing in its implication that if men persist in trying to "conquer" women, to exploit them "in the eternal war—the war between men and women," women will eventually act in what they perceive as self-defense (96). Austin does not judge Dulcie Adelaid's action. She presents considerable justification for it in the discussions between Dulcie and Arliss in the desert. Perhaps most significantly, after Dulcie Adelaid loses her innocence and confronts and kills the snake that had entered her Eden, Austin allows her to escape to the West, to a world we recognize will heal her.

Ironically, Dulcie can escape because she, like so many women, has been expunged from the public record, while Arliss becomes a legend, the real meaning of his death lost. As she does in many stories, Austin shows how women's stories, lives, and values are lost, obliterated by the male text.[11] But like Dulcie, Austin is a skilled tracker, and *Cactus Thorn* follows the trail of the lost story. While for Arliss the woman has existed only in relation to him and his needs, the inevitable narrative shift from Arliss to Dulcie in the story's final paragraph and the clear sympathy for her in the story's last line *finally* acknowledge her centrality to the story. For if this is a story about how to "live sincerely," Dulcie Adelaid and not Grant Arliss is its hero.

In fact, Austin had been tracking characters like Dulcie from the beginning of her career, independent farseeing women who, like their creator, believed that the desert uncramps the soul and provides the space to walk off society-made values. Austin called such women "chiseras," and their trails wander throughout her fiction. Such women become Austin's prophets, often inspiring other women, as the Walking Woman inspires the narrator. Remembering the local rumors that the Walking Woman is "twisted," the narrator of the story looks at her footsteps and discovers that "the track of her two feet bore evenly and white" ("The Walking Woman," 98);[12] by concluding with this metaphor, Austin reminds her readers to seek their own "reading" of any story and stresses the Walking Woman's role as spiritual leader. Austin's chiseras are her most memorable and original characters, reflecting her encounters as a young woman with Paiute women, who taught her the meaning of art, and embodying her own beliefs and conflicts.

Although Austin's chiseras are surely descended from Sarah Orne Jewett's Mrs. Todd, an herbalist and a seer, she saw them as rooted in the West. In one of her earliest pieces, Austin paid tribute to the original chisera, Seyavi, "The Basketmaker," from whom she learned what she called her "naked craft. . . . Learning that, she learned to write" (*Earth Horizon*, 289). Hearing that Austin's daughter Ruth could not speak, Sevayi brought her friend meadowlarks' tongues "which make the speech nimble and quick"; they could not help Ruth, who was severely retarded, but Seyavi's many gifts inspired Austin to discover her own way to speak (*Earth Horizon*, 246). She was impressed with Seyavi's skill at weaving nature and culture into a unified design which expresses her "humanity," and her baskets became emblems of art's source, "the satisfaction of desire" ("The Basket Maker," 33).[13] But the Paiutes also taught her a broader definition of art.

Mary would see the [Paiute] women moving across the mesa on pleasant days, digging wild hyacinth roots, seed-gathering, and . . . would often join them, absorbing women's lore, plants good to be eaten or for medicine, learning to make snares of long, strong hair for the quail, . . . how and when to gather willows and cedar roots for basket-making. It was in this fashion that she began to learn that to get at the meaning of work you must make all its motions, both of body and mind. It was one of the activities which has had continuing force throughout her life. (*Earth Horizon*, 246–47)

Seyavi and the Paiutes taught Austin that art is a process of living, the artist one who "sees, feels, creates" the patterns of human existence, who can "interpret the significance of common things," who can integrate the domestic life with the individual vision of the artist ("The Basket Maker," 32; *Earth Horizon*, 362).

These qualities also belong to Dulcie. Austin once wrote that "what women have to stand on squarely [is] not their ability to see the world in the way men see it, but the importance and validity of seeing it in some other way" (*The Young Woman Citizen*, 19),[14] and much of *Cactus Thorn* is devoted to Dulcie's way of seeing. Her philosophy of living sincerely is based on her spiritual integration with the land, and she tests her beliefs against her observations of nature around her. The desert teaches her to think for herself rather than in "made-up" or inherited ways. She trusts the evidence of personal experience, and like Seyavi, she sees to the "bare core of things." Because she is receptive to "It," to the desert's energy, she has the flame of inspiration Arliss so wants to possess. Although Austin never directly identifies Dulcie as creating art, her way of seeing and her creative force, so in harmony with the desert's power, reveal her to be an artist, a seer—and, in many ways, a reflection of her creator.

Like the Walking Woman's footprints, certain themes track

through many Austin stories, and she sets Dulcie Adelaid off
on one such trail, on a search for a relationship with a man as
passionate and intense as her love for the land and for her artistic
vision. In Austin's fiction this trail inevitably forks, and because
her independent heroines never abandon the road less traveled
by, they are denied the more conventional path to love and
happy marriage. The real choice, Austin suggests, belongs to the
man. "Marry me—and my work," says Olivia Lattimore in *A
Woman of Genius*, and in response her lover chooses a conventional
woman who will be a suitable stepmother to his children, as
Arliss chooses a woman who can advance his career. "[I]f only
I could have [my husband] and my work," Olivia exclaims, "I
should ask no more of destiny; I do not now see why I couldn't."[15]
Austin was never able to resolve that problem, but many of her
stories address it. *Cactus Thorn* can be read as a retelling of one
such story, "The Coyote-Spirit and the Weaving Woman" (1904),
which provides a rich context in which to understand Dulcie
Adelaid's dilemmas—and Mary Austin's.

"The Coyote-Spirit and the Weaving Woman" is a western tall
tale from a woman's point of view; it values emotional rather than
physical strength and suggests that imaginative exploration of
the landscape is far more empowering than the attempt to possess territory and keep others out of it. With her "infirmity of
the eyes," the Weaving Woman is "different from other people"
because her vision is larger. "Because there was nobody found
who wished to live with her," she "lived alone" in the wilderness
"weaving patterns in her baskets of all that she saw or thought"
("The Coyote-Spirit . . . ," 114, 116).[16] Her art reveals the rich-
ness of her imagination and experience, causing others "as they
stroked the perfect curves of the bowls or traced out the patterns"
to think "how fine life would be if it were so rich and bright as she
made it seem, instead of the dull occasion they had found it."
The Weaving Woman sees more than others because she is re-

sponsive to nature and its mysteries: "the wild things showed her many a wonder hid from those who have not rainbow fringes to their eyes." "[N]ot afraid of anything," she is a wanderer, who "went farther and farther into the silent places until . . . she met the Coyote-Spirit" ("The Coyote-Spirit . . . ," 114).

In her parable, Austin suggests the conflicts within the male psyche by creating a character who is half-man, half-coyote. She makes him a comic figure, a descendant of the fairy tale wolf, who plans to "devour" the Weaving Woman, but he is also threatening, his "appetites" clearly sexual metaphors. When the Weaving Woman wanders into his range, he thinks she must "expect to take the consequences" ("The Coyote-Spirit . . . ," 115). His coyote side expresses the violence and possessiveness often associated with the western male, but the Weaving Woman laughs at his blustering, insisting he is "only a man." She forces him to acknowledge his humanity, and the two establish a bond. But though his sexual attraction to her remains strong, he responds by marrying the Goat Girl, the "right sort of a girl," who had "always stayed in the safe open places and gone home early" ("The Coyote-Spirit . . . ," 118).

With her family connections and social graces, Alida Rittenhouse may initially seem quite distanced from the Goat Girl, but she is, of course, a recasting of the same character, the woman who never wanders beyond the "safe open places." Through characters like the Weaving Woman and Dulcie Adelaid, Austin explores what nontraditional women can offer men: not only a sexual intensity but also a richer vision of human possibility. Like the women they ultimately choose, these men are not comfortable in the secret places in the wilderness, Austin's metaphor for female passion and for the search for spiritual meaning. Once having "possessed" the women and the wilderness, they abandon them and marry the women who represent their own "desire" for safety and security. Unlike Dulcie, the Weaving Woman ignores the Coyote-Spirit's rejection and goes on with her weaving, but because her basket patterns express all she saw or felt, we can assume that her loneliness is "written" into them. The difference in the endings of "The Coyote-Spirit and the Weaving Woman" and *Cactus Thorn* may represent the effects of nearly twenty-five years of frequently bitter experience. Then again, the Weaving Woman's story may reinforce the sense that once Dulcie returns to the desert and her activities there, she will be healed.

That men like the Coyote-Spirit and Grant Arliss see the world as made up of two "sorts" of women reveals the limitations of their thinking, where things are one thing or another but never both. Austin's chiseras have perhaps been so long overlooked, despite their appeal and power, because they do not readily fit into any of our inherited ways of thinking about western women's lives: like the classic hero of western literature, they head into the wilderness in search of their own moral values, but they do not reject their womanhood, or the home and the hearth; they are rebels, but they do not try to outdo men at their own game. It is no wonder that Arliss and the Coyote-Spirit have difficulty understanding these women; they have been granted no place within our culture. Despite Arliss's efforts, Dulcie cannot readily be categorized. Like other Austin characters, she is *both* self-sufficient and lonely, independent and vulnerable to men, gentle and dangerous, a wanderer concerned with the domestic beauty of everyday life. The desert has given her psychological and spiritual resources, and she belongs in the wilderness.

Much of *Cactus Thorn*'s beauty lies in Austin's evocation of Dulcie Adelaid's sexuality, emotions, and character through natural imagery and symbols. The depth of her nature is suggested, for instance, by her source, her birthplace, a fertile spring, Sweetwater, *Agua Dulce*, an image which also evokes her sexuality, her intimacy with nature. The sexual image is subtly—and ironically—reinforced when Dulcie comments that "snakes were so much more likely to be found in the neighborhood of water-holes" (47). *Cactus Thorn*, so different in style from the books of the New York years, has "the mark of the land" upon it; in it Austin returned to the lyrical style of her desert works, where she had used female metaphors to describe the land while exploring the inner reality of her women characters through natural descriptions, works which showed the influence of Jewett and which, in turn, may well have influenced the work of Austin's friend Willa Cather.[17]

Through developing the parallels between Dulcie and the land, Austin examines the parallels between men's desire to conquer and use the land and to possess women. Because he has lost his ties to the earth, Arliss can experience the vital connections between nature and the spirit, between passion and creativity, only through a woman; she becomes a vehicle, a "sheath," for him "to impenetrate," valuable only for what she can make him feel. Austin contrasts those desires to Dulcie's belief that life's meaning can be found only through receptivity. The land teaches Dulcie that power comes through working with a force, not trying to control it—and never abandoning it. Thus Austin implies that Dulcie, like the land, has a "natural" right to fight back in order to heal herself. Although she makes Dulcie's lonely passion for Arliss convincing, she also makes the reader feel more powerfully her emotional and sexual bond to the land. She leaves no doubt that of her two lovers, Dulcie ends up with the proper one.

Austin may well have conceived Dulcie's escape to the healing West as an echo of her own escape from the city to a sanctuary where it was possible to live sincerely. Dulcie Adelaid's story can be read as a reflection of Austin's personal life in other ways, as well. Like Dulcie, she needed to rid herself of a man, and she must have felt a sense of relief in killing him off. Had *Cactus Thorn* been published when it was written in 1927, Lincoln

Steffens, the muckraking journalist and author of *The Shame of the Cities* (1904), might have spent the rest of his life looking over his shoulder.

Austin met Steffens, a political reformer like Arliss, in 1906 or 1907, shortly after she had left her husband and joined the artist community at Carmel.[18] He was likely the model for the sociologist Herman in her utopian fantasy, *Outland* (1910), a reformer who is the too "reasonable" love interest of the heroine, an English professor.[19] In her autobiography, *Earth Horizon*, Austin wrote that unlike earlier feminists such as Frances Willard, who recognized the necessity of making a conscious choice between career and marriage, feminists of her generation believed that marriage could be "remedied," and she hoped to find a man whose commitment to a "new marriage" matched her own, "a man who was big enough so I couldn't walk all around him, so to speak,—somebody that I could reach and reach and not find the end of" ("Frustrate," 233). When she moved to New York, she and Steffens had an affair, and for a time he apparently seemed like such a man. She was flattered that he admired her writings, and she began her New York notebook from 1911 with a passage which implies her attraction to him:

> I have opened this account at the insistence of my friend Lincoln Steffens to prove to him that I can not write a book about the city as interesting as *The Land of Little Rain*. Steffy is saturated with the city. He can look at his watch any time of day and tell you what is going on in any part of it at that particular hour, and he can't understand that it will take me more years to learn my way about in it than were necessary to know the trails from Mojave to Lone Pine.[20]

In 1911, Steffens took up with another woman before ending his relationship with Austin, and she was badly hurt, angry at what she considered the hypocritical contradictions between his behavior and his beliefs. Ironically, she presented a nasty critique of him as Adam Frear, the socialist editor of *The Proletariat*, in *No. 26 Jayne Street*, a novel "saturated with the city" he had urged her to write about, an urban novel about sex, class, and politics from an iconoclastic feminist stance, an interesting companion piece to *Cactus Thorn*.

The novel explores relations between men and women within the context of war, strikes, and political unrest in a New York caught up in public arguments about feminism, socialism, and capitalism. Its young heroine, Neith Schuyler, finds herself lost in a maze of conflicting philosophies, and eventually she falls in love with the charismatic Frear. Initially she "translated all the large-mindedness of Adam Frear's political outlook into terms of personal living, when, as a matter of fact, he wrote of men in nations. He dealt with parties and policies and she thought of men and women" (*No. 26 Jayne Street*, 170).[21] He is contrasted with another character to whom Neith is attracted, Rose Matlock, a feminist speaker who connects the public and the private, the abstract and the personal:

> All our language of sex is phrased in the terms of war, of strategy, of maneuvers, surprises. . . . We talk of conquest, of winning and being won. We cannot come together for the purpose of increasing our kind without a treaty of peace between the protagonists. Contracts hedged about with reprisals and indemnities . . . And without that contract we fail to respect ourselves and one another. (*No. 26 Jayne Street*, 126)

When Neith realizes that Frear has asked her to marry him before breaking off a secret relationship with Rose, she questions why he does not see the disjunction between his challenges to capitalism and his view that "a woman was a secondary thing" (*No. 26 Jayne Street*, 327). Adam's behavior seems to her "familiar ground" shared with men whose politics he supposedly rejects:

> . . . his passions ran neck and neck with Bruce Havens's greed in the "business" game, and the Senator's crass appetite for power. Here he unleashed himself to the old tricks and evasions, the unrestricted play of selfness in the personal relations. (*No. 26 Jayne Street*, 327)

Realizing that "what Adam Frear and his friends looked forward to was the mere shift of the accent of autocracy," Neith decides that she cannot forgive him for his "offense . . . against another woman" (*No. 26 Jayne Street*, 298, 342). While Neith might easily have played the role of Alida Rittenhouse or the Goat Girl, Austin presents her with a choice. She breaks their engagement and prepares herself to find work that will give her life meaning. Like Dulcie, she seeks a way to live sincerely.

Austin recreated Adam Frear in Grant Arliss because she was not yet through with him. A passage she wrote a few years before her death underscores her personal reasons for writing and rewriting the story of the radical man unwilling to examine his attitudes toward women: as she considered her marriage and her love affairs she gradually came to believe that "there is a male incapacity for re-patterning the personal life which is insuperable":

> It cropped up in other men whom I might possibly have married. Twice I was near it, but felt . . . inhibited by the incapacity of the men involved for making the adjustment. They could not come even halfway, as men of a younger generation have done. . . . [The] men who might have married me were of the intellectual class, often involved in creative careers, and not financially secure. One or the other

of us would have to make sacrifices; and it was always
sufficiently plain that I should have to be the one. (*Earth
Horizon*, 350)

I have no doubt that Austin recognized and took pleasure in
the psychological symbolism of her "murder" of Arliss, but if
she wrote about the personal, she recognized its political implications. Like many of her feminist themes, her treatment of the
power dynamics between women and men transcends generations: women often encountered such men in the civil rights and
antiwar movements of the 1960s and, I dare say, there are some
around today. Although *Cactus Thorn* is an angry work, Austin
never gave up on men: she had a satisfying affair with a botanist,
Daniel T. MacDougal, in the 1920s, and she wrote a novel after
Cactus Thorn, Starry Adventure (1931), in which a self-aware male
protagonist tries to create an egalitarian marriage, the kind of
marriage she had envisioned at the end of *A Woman of Genius*.
Like the Weaving Woman and Dulcie Adelaid, Austin tried to
see more in men than they saw in themselves. She hoped and
believed that someday the language of conquering and warfare
would disappear.

Austin's work does not provide further ammunition for the
"battle of the sexes," but an analysis intended to help end it.
"Civilization as we now have it," she said, "is one-eyed and one-
handed. It is kept going by man's way of dealing with the things
he sees" (*The Young Woman Citizen*, 17). While Austin sometimes
pointed out the limitations in "man's way of seeing," she granted
the male point of view legitimacy, only wanting society to have
the benefit of two hands. *Cactus Thorn* demonstrates why Austin
deserves acknowledgment as an influential feminist thinker, a
woman who throughout her career argued for "the importance
and validity of seeing the world in some other way."

Austin described the genesis of this vision in *Earth Horizon*. She said that she "was never much taken with the wish of many girls of her acquaintance that they had been boys." She "thought there might be a great deal to be got out of being a woman; but she definitely meant neither to chirrup nor twitter." She "meant not to remit a single flash of wit, anger, or imagination." She "had no idea of what, in her time, such a determination would entail" and "was but dimly aware of something within herself, competent, self-directive; she meant to trust it" (*Earth Horizon*, 157–58). Unwilling to borrow a male point of view or to accept the chirrups and twitters expected of the woman writer, Austin saw the liberation of her "wit, anger, [and] imagination" as central to understanding what was "to be got out of being a woman."

Her life she saw as an opportunity to "help other women to speak out what they think, unashamed" (*A Woman of Genius*, 503). In many works she put forth a feminist agenda for social change called "Woman Thought." The truths she revealed have become central to feminist writers today. Like Dulcie, who acknowledged her ties to her mother through taking her name, Austin explored her mother's life to understand its centrality to her identity. While she exposed the narrowness of her culture's idea of "true womanliness," as she called it, she paid tribute to the power of women's culture and the value of women's traditional domestic role. "Women, in their hundred thousand years of managing the family," she said, "have developed a genius for personal relations," a genius for cooperation and affiliation that should be put to use for the public good.[22] At the same time she argued that the "traditional . . . structure of married life [is based on] the pattern of male dominance and feminine subservience," that women must have the opportunity for meaningful work outside the home and the "courage to live lives of their own" (*Earth Horizon*, 271; *A Woman of Genius*, 451). She chal-

lenged the portrayal of women in works by male writers and revealed how gender roles handicap both women and men. She
wrote women's history, defining the special concerns of different
generations of women and their contributions to society. In *The
Young Woman Citizen*, she encouraged young women to see their
unique contributions to politics. "I have always believed," she
said, "that there is a distinctly feminine approach to intellectual
problems and its recognition is indispensible to intellectual whole-
ness. All that I have ever, as a feminist, protected against, is the
prevailing notion that the feminine is necessarily an inferior
approach."[23]

In *Cactus Thorn*, Austin certainly liberated a woman's wit,
anger, and imagination. Threatening, unnerving, original, it is a
sister text to "A Jury of Her Peers" and to "The Yellow Wall-
paper," by Austin's friend, Charlotte Perkins Gilman, to Elizabeth Stuart Phelps's *The Story of Avis*, Mary Wilkins Freeman's
"The Revolt of Mother," and her own *A Woman of Genius*. Like
these feminist classics, *Cactus Thorn* blends the lyrical and the
political; like them, it is daring in its ironic treatment of male attitudes and its willingness to express a uniquely female way of
seeing; its voice, like theirs, was for many years unheard.

In *No. 26 Jayne Street*, Austin described her feeling that women
had been silenced by a "wall of men, a filtered, almost sound-
proof wall of male intelligence, male reporters, critics, managers,
advertisers . . . men editors, men publishers, men reviewers"
(*No. 26 Jayne Street*, 6). *Cactus Thorn* was rejected by Ferris
Greenslet of Houghton Mifflin because "the hero's defection and
his subsequent murder by the lady are not made absolutely convincing"; but a note Austin left on another of her unpublished
stories is perhaps more revealing: ". . . rejected by many editors
as too 'radical.'"[24] It is a pleasure to hear Austin speak once
again, after long silence.

Notes

1. Unless otherwise indicated, page numbers cited in the Afterword refer to *Cactus Thorn*.

2. Austin knew and worked with Ida Tarbell, Emma Goldman, Charlotte Perkins Gilman, Margaret Sanger, and Elizabeth Gurley Flynn. She was a friend or acquaintance of a host of New York writers and intellectuals such as Vachel Lindsay, Carl Van Doren, and Willa Cather.

3. Mary Austin, *Earth Horizon* (New York: Literary Guild, 1932).

4. Many characters in Austin's collection *Lost Borders* (1909) carry the "mark of the land"; the phrase occurs in the introductory sketch to the collection, "The Land," included in *Western Trails: A Collection of Stories by Mary Austin*, ed. Melody Graulich (Reno and Las Vegas: University of Nevada Press, 1987), p. 44. See the introduction to *Western Trails* for a more detailed description of Austin's life and writing.

5. "The Land," in *Western Trails*.

6. Although Austin treats Native Americans as background characters and servants in *Cactus Thorn*, many of her other works explore Native American art, culture, and beliefs with great sympathy. Although she did not entirely escape the racial stereotypes of her time, she was a lifelong advocate for Indian rights.

7. "The Walking Woman," in *Western Trails*.

8. Originally published in *The Century Magazine* in 1912, "Frustrate" is reprinted in *Western Trails*.

9. See Annette Kolodny's *The Lay of the Land* (Chapel Hill: University of North Carolina Press, 1975) for an analysis of the American male writer's use of sexual imagery in describing the American landscape; in many ways, Austin's analysis can be seen as anticipating Kolodny's. Kolodny's second book, *The Land Be-*

fore Her (Chapel Hill: University of North Carolina Press, 1984), which explores women writers' descriptions of the West, provides a historical context for Dulcie Adelaid's views.

10. Mary Austin, *Love and the Soul-Maker* (New York: D. Appleton and Company, 1914), pp. 231–32.

11. See, for example, two wonderful stories from *Lost Borders*, "The Woman at the Eighteen-Mile" and "The Return of Mr. Wills," both included in *Western Trails*.

12. "The Walking Woman," in *Western Trails*.

13. "The Basket-Maker," in *Western Trails*.

14. Mary Austin, *The Young Woman Citizen* (New York: Woman's Press, 1918).

15. *A Woman of Genius* (Garden City, N.J.: Doubleday, Page, and Company, 1912), p. 191. The Feminist Press has recently reissued *A Woman of Genius*, with a fine afterword by Nancy Porter.

In *A Woman of Genius*, Olivia says she writes her story to make "things easier for women who must tread my path of work and loneliness" (503). In *Earth Horizon*, Austin used a similar metaphor to explain her estrangement with her marriage: she described the "more or less secret antagonism" between her husband and herself during their "excursions to the wild," an antagonism "which grew out of [her husband's] native unwillingness toward coöperative activity, a deeply cherished instinct for selfness. He was not only happier to plan a trail for himself, but to break it at his own instigation" (*Earth Horizon*, 288). Her most persistent complaint about the relations between women and men was that in marriage both society and husbands expected wives to give up their own explorations, to follow always, literally and metaphorically, in the husband's footsteps, no matter where they might lead.

16. "The Coyote-Spirit and the Weaving Woman," in *Western Trails*.

17. Austin mentioned reading Jewett in *Earth Horizon*, and Cather paid tribute to Austin in a personal inscription to a gift of *Death Comes for the Archbishop*, now owned by The Huntington Library.

18. See Augusta Fink, *I-Mary: A Biography of Mary Austin* (Tucson: The University of Arizona Press, 1983), for a fuller discussion of this meeting.

19. T. M. Pearce first noted this similarity in his editorial notes to *Literary America 1903–1934: The Mary Austin Letters* (Westport, Conn.: Greenwood Press, 1979).

20. The Huntington Library owns Austin's New York notebook, which can be found in Box 24C. A long letter Steffens wrote to Austin in 1911 suggests why she would have found him attractive:

> [I have] a deep sympathy for the feeling you express [of needing to write to someone who would understand], and I wish you to know that I shall read all that you care to write, especially in that mood, with more understanding than may appear. For I think I can understand. I certainly want to understand. I'd rather a thousand times understand than be understood. . . . I must say to you sincerely, and earnestly, that if you wish to put yourself down on paper you may do so with me and be sure, oh, absolutely sure, that you will be read as I would be read—with the wish only to understand. (Quoted in *Literary America*, p. 43)

21. Mary Austin, *No. 26 Jayne Street* (Boston: Houghton Mifflin Co., 1920).

22. "Woman Looks at Her World," *Pictorial Review* (November 1924), p. 69.

23. Austin made this comment in a letter to *The New Republic* about a review by Lewis Mumford of her work *American Rhythm*.

The clipping is contained in The Huntington Library's Austin collection, Box 25.

24. Greenslet wrote Austin on July 25, 1927; the letter is contained in The Huntington Library's Austin collection, Box 12. The story is "Kate Bixby's Queerness," located in Box 41 of The Huntington Library's Austin collection and reprinted in *Western Trails*.

Designed by Richard Hendel

Text set in Janson with display in Greco Deco

Composed by G & S Typesetters, Austin, Texas

Printed and bound by Malloy Lithographing, Ann Arbor, Michigan